MW01169309

TORRENTS OF FEAR

LANTERN BEACH ROMANTIC SUSPENSE,
BOOK 6

CHRISTY BARRITT

CHANGE CHAPTER ONE

"I'M GOING to play you a little ditty about what it's like to have loved and lost," Carter Denver murmured into the microphone. "I'm sure nobody here understands that, do you?"

A round of chuckles went through the crowd of one hundred or so people who'd gathered around Carter on a small covered stage near the Lantern Beach boardwalk.

He was a one-man show. Just him, his guitar, and the songs he'd written.

This was the way he preferred it. He liked doing music on his terms.

He strummed his guitar, finding his key before launching into the ballad he'd written called "Requiem of Love." As he opened his mouth to croon the first verse, he scanned the crowd, pleased at their apt attention.

It was October here in North Carolina, and the sky was already dark. Lights had been set up to illuminate the stage area, but the dimness gave everything an intimate feeling. That, mixed with the salty scent of the ocean, made for a perfect evening.

Carter was doing this show as a part of a late season concert series. Every Friday night, a different artist took to the small stage and entertained any locals or tourists on the island who wanted a night out on the town.

He didn't mind. In fact, he loved this island and the people here. He could often be found playing in local restaurants or singing the national anthem at high school football games. The slower-paced life fit him.

As Carter glanced through the crowd, his gaze stopped at someone standing at the back.

He stumbled over the lyrics before quickly recovering. Probably no one noticed—nobody but him. He hit the next chord, on autopilot as he continued singing.

But Carter couldn't pull his gaze from who he thought he'd seen.

Carter's eyes must be playing tricks on him.

Maybe it was the darkness. Maybe it was the distance.

Because there was no way he'd seen the person he thought he had.

Still singing, Carter searched the crowd again.

But the woman was gone.

Probably because she had never been there.

Or, more likely, this person had simply resembled someone from his past. In the dusk and with the shadows, her face had morphed to look like someone familiar.

His racing pulse slowed some at the realization.

Carter moved on to the second verse, back in the moment. He had the audience's complete attention, and that was one of the greatest honors he could achieve.

His favorite thing to do was tell stories with songs. He wasn't the type of singer who'd ever draw large crowds in stadiums. No, he was more of a Simon and Garfunkel type. He never wanted to change. This was who he was.

Just as he was about to start the chorus again, the woman at the back of the crowd came into view again.

His voice caught when he saw her.

A few people on the front row murmured

amongst themselves. It wasn't like Carter to mess up. People who came to each of his concerts knew that.

But he couldn't look away.

He'd seen the woman again.

This time he'd gotten a better look at her.

She'd been staring right at Carter, almost as if she'd come here looking for him.

But that couldn't be the case.

It couldn't be Allison Daniels.

Because Allison was dead.

CHAPTER TWO

CARTER BARELY MANAGED to finish the song. But he did. He was a professional, and he needed to act like it.

As soon as the last note finished ringing out, he set his guitar back into the stand beside him and grabbed a bottle of water.

He leaned toward the microphone in front of him. "I need to take a ten-minute break. But I hope to see you back here in a few minutes."

Before he could question his decision, he hurried off the small stage.

Carter needed to find that woman. He needed to know the truth or the unknown would always haunt him.

He glanced through the crowd. Several people

had slipped away to get concessions from a few businesses that remained open nearby.

Where had the woman gone?

Carter had looked away for only a moment, but it must have been enough time for her to disappear again.

She couldn't have gotten too far.

"Hey, Carter—" someone in the crowd tried to stop him.

"One minute," Carter muttered, hoping he didn't seem rude as he hurried past.

But time was of the essence here. He couldn't let this woman slip away. He'd never be at peace with himself if he didn't try to find answers right now.

He continued to scan everything around him. The shops on the boardwalk. A little amusement park with its colorful Ferris wheel. Wooden bench swings along the ocean that swayed in the breeze.

But no Allison.

He paused on the wooden boardwalk that flanked the sandy shores of the Atlantic Ocean and glanced to the left.

No sign of her.

He glanced to the right.

No sign of her—

Wait.

Could that be Allison up ahead?

The figure in the distance scurried away.

The blonde hair was the same. The lithe build matched Allison's. Even the style of clothing—tight jeans with a loose-fitting white top—looked like something Allison would wear.

Carter had to catch her.

Now.

As if the woman sensed he was there, she looked back over her shoulder. Her eyes widened when she spotted Carter behind her.

"Hey!" he called, waving a hand in the air to stop her.

Instead, she took off in a run.

In a run? Why would she do that?

It didn't matter.

The woman was supposed to be dead.

Carter had no idea what was going on here. But he intended to find out.

He took off after her.

The woman glanced over her shoulder again and sprinted faster.

He couldn't let her get away.

She cut to the left and into a narrow alley between two buildings.

Carter chased after her, turning into the dark corridor.

He didn't see her.

She must have already reached the other end.

He picked up his pace, determined to find her.

But just as he reached the corner of the building, something hard hit his head.

And everything went black as he collapsed.

———

"CARTER? CARTER? ARE YOU OKAY?"

Carter jerked his eyes open, a terrible throb at the back of his head.

Slowly, Ty Chambers came into view. His friend knelt over him, concern lacing his eyes.

As Carter glanced around, he saw he was in an alley near the boardwalk. The sky was dark. The crowds sounded distant.

Everything rushed back to him. Allison. Chasing her. Feeling something hit him.

His head pounded harder at the memories.

Carter lifted a hand and rubbed his temples, trying to form a coherent thought. "I think...I think I'm okay."

"Can you sit up?"

Carter nodded.

Ty offered his hand and pulled Carter upright.

His head wobbled.

As soon as his world righted again, he let his friend help him to his feet. Even as Carter stood, Ty hovered close, just in case he needed a hand.

"Everyone is looking for you," Ty said. "You didn't come back to start your next set and people became worried. Cassidy and I split up to see if we could find you. She's on her way here now."

Carter waved him off. "I'm fine. I didn't mean for anyone to make a big deal out of me leaving. I'll go back and finish my set."

Ty narrowed his eyes, still studying him. "There's no need for that. Most people have already left. It's been twenty minutes, and people just assumed you weren't coming back."

"Oh, man. Twenty minutes?" Carter shook his head. He'd really been out that long? "I'm so sorry. That wasn't what I meant to happen."

Just then, Cassidy, Ty's wife, appeared. Not only was she a friend, but Cassidy was also the police chief here in town.

"Carter," she murmured, offering the same scrutiny as Ty had while she hovered in front of him.

"I'm so glad we found you. I was getting worried. What happened?"

He considered what he might say. There were parts of his past he didn't want anyone to know about. Not even his friends. But he didn't want to lie either. He'd concealed the person he used to be for so long . . . he hated to bring that person back into the light.

"I thought I saw someone I knew." Carter decided to stick to a simplified version of the truth. "I wandered out here to find her, and, the next thing I knew, something hit me on the back of the head. Everything went black and now . . . here you are."

Cassidy looked around and nodded toward an old crowbar lying near a trashcan beside the building. "They could have used this. I'll take it to the station and check it for prints."

"You don't have to do that." He never meant to make a big deal out of this.

Cassidy's eyes narrowed as if she was trying to figure him out. "I think I should. Someone assaulted you, Carter. That's serious."

He waved her off, trying to pretend like this wasn't anything to be concerned about. But another part of him wanted to know whose prints might be on that crowbar. A war raged inside him.

"You know what? I thought I saw an old friend, but it wasn't. The woman was a stranger. She probably thought some creepy man was chasing her through a dark alley. I can't blame her for hitting me over the head." Carter tried to let out a chuckle, but it sounded strangled.

Cassidy and Ty continued to study him, as if trying to ascertain his state of mind.

"I'm with Cassidy," Ty said. "Maybe we should take you to the clinic to be checked out, just to be on the safe side."

Carter rubbed the back of his head again. "I'm fine. It's just my pride that's injured. I never intended for people to get worried, and I'm a little embarrassed, to be truthful. Best thing I can do probably is to go back to my place and get a little rest."

Cassidy and Ty still stared at him as if they weren't sure his words were true.

"Going to sleep is probably not the best thing you can do in case you have a concussion," Cassidy said.

"You're right," Carter said. "But I have some music I'm working on. It won't be a problem to stay awake. Bo will make sure to keep me awake." Bo was his dog—a four-year-old German shepherd that loved to take walks, chew bones, and who snored like a freight train when he slept.

"Are you sure?" Ty said. "I can go over and hang out with you for a while."

Carter shook his head, instantly regretting the action. Not only was he dizzy, but he was going to be sore. A knot the size of a golf ball had already formed on the back of his head. As he reached behind him, he could feel it. "No, really. I'm fine."

"How about if we get your equipment for you and swing it by your apartment?" Cassidy said. "That way you can get back home. You look like you might need a moment to yourself."

Gratitude filled him. A moment to himself was *exactly* what he needed.

Because Carter couldn't get the image of Allison scurrying down the boardwalk out of his mind.

Nor the fact that her familiar jasmine and almond perfume seemed to be lingering in the air.

CHAPTER THREE

CARTER SLOUCHED in the oversized leather chair in the corner of his living room. He'd dimmed the lights around him as he stared at the cell phone in his hands.

Did he really want to do this?

He'd been thinking about it for the past hour.

If that wasn't a sign, he didn't know what was.

Letting out one more breath, he finally dialed the number he'd been contemplating.

A moment later, a familiar voice came on the line. "Carter? Is that you?"

Carter felt himself relax as soon as he realized who was on the other end. "Hey, Sadie. Yes, it's me. Carter."

"I haven't talked to you in ages," she rushed, her

voice as soothing and kind as always. "What's going on? I think about you all the time. I wonder how you're doing. But after what happened . . . you stopped returning my calls. So I figured . . . never mind. How are you?"

Guilt flooded him. Sadie was right. Carter *hadn't* returned her calls. He didn't think he could handle talking to her. Not when his pain was so fresh.

But now that he was facing this crisis, Sadie was the only person he wanted to turn to.

"I'm . . . I've done better," he finally said, deciding not to skirt around the truth.

Some of the warmth disappeared from her voice, replaced with concern. "Is everything okay? What's going on?"

He ran a hand over his face, trying to pull his thoughts together and to swallow enough of his pride to share what he needed to share. "I don't know how to ask you this, Sadie, except just to come right out and do it. I need to see you."

"Need to see me? That's something I never thought I'd hear."

"I know." Carter's voice broke, and he ran his hand over his face again.

It wasn't too late to back out of this. To tell her this was a misunderstanding or to make up an excuse. But he couldn't do that. Too much was at stake.

"You're worrying me, Carter."

"It's just . . ." How did he even say this? "You're the only person I can think of who could help me, who might . . . understand."

"Are you asking me this as a therapist or as a friend?"

He swallowed hard as his throat began to tighten with emotion. "As a friend. I'm asking you to come as a friend, Sadie."

"I'll be there as soon as I can."

SADIE THOMPSON GRIPPED the steering wheel, her thoughts racing as she headed down the road.

The last person she ever thought she'd hear from was Carter Denver.

The two of them went back nearly fifteen years.

Carter, Allison, and Sadie . . . they'd all been inseparable during high school and college. They said they would always be a threesome—best friends for life.

Then Carter and Allison began to date. For a

long time, Sadie had been like a third wheel, but, despite that, they'd all remained friends.

Until things between Carter and Allison fell apart.

Then, after Allison died, Carter had pulled away completely, acting almost like he wanted to forget about those chapters of his life—chapters that included not only Allison but Sadie also.

Sadie had assumed that when Carter saw her, it brought back too many memories about what had happened. She could understand that. The past . . . it was painful. Brutal, at times. Moving beyond it was like climbing a mountain—it required effort and time, and there weren't any shortcuts.

That's what she always told her clients. She understood because she'd lived it.

She glanced at the digital clock in her car.

Three a.m.

Sadie kept driving. She'd been able to clear her schedule fairly easily. It was one of the blessings of working for herself. She knew enough to know when a friend was in crisis.

Carter was definitely in crisis right now.

Tears blinded her eyes, but she quickly waved them away. Closing the door on that chapter of her life had caused so much heartache. Sure, she'd moved on. She'd become a professional life coach and worked with many well-known singers in Nashville. She'd established a new life with new friends and new accomplishments.

But it was as if a part of her heart had been ripped out never to be replaced when her friendship with Carter died. She'd grieved. Oh, how she'd grieved and mourned the loss. The ending was so abrupt that Carter might as well have been dead.

Sadie pulled off the interstate and onto a back road headed toward Lantern Beach, North Carolina. She still wasn't sure why her friend had decided to settle down on the isolated island, but something about it must have captured his attention. From what she'd heard, the area was beautiful.

It was a long drive from Nashville. She knew from the quick research she'd done that she still had to catch a couple of ferries until she would get to the isolated island. At the earliest, it would be morning before she saw Carter.

She hoped he would be okay in the meantime. But she'd heard the anguish in his voice. Allison's death had nearly torn him apart. At best, it had made him disappear. At worst, he'd become a shell of who he'd been.

Carter was one of the most talented men Sadie

had ever met. She hated to see him bury his talent like he had.

She only hoped that whatever he was going through now, she would be able to help him work through it.

CHAPTER FOUR

AS PROMISED, Carter had kept himself awake all night. It wasn't incredibly hard for him considering he was a musician and did some of his best work while the rest of the world slept.

Just as the sun broke over the horizon, a knock sounded at his front door.

He wasn't sure exactly whom he expected to see on the other side. Sometimes, the man who owned the fudge shop downstairs stopped by with samples. Other times, the boy down the street came to see if Carter needed him to walk Bo. Or it could be Cassidy and Ty coming to check on him again.

When Carter pulled the door open, his eyes widened at the person standing there.

"Sadie?" The word almost sounded breathless as it left his lips.

She held up a bag in her hands. "I bring good tidings of great doughnuts."

Carter continued to stare at her, barely hearing what she had to say.

He couldn't believe that Sadie was here. Already. He figured the earliest she might arrive would be this evening. She must have driven all night.

Carter drank her in. She looked great. Better than he even remembered, with her long, light brown hair that flowed in waves down her back, her peaches and cream complexion, and her wide smile.

He remembered his manners and stepped forward, wrapping his arms around her. "I can't believe you're here."

Peaches and cream. Not only did that phrase match her complexion, but it also matched the way she smelled. Like fresh fruit. Like sweetness.

Feeling Sadie's arms around him made Carter feel more at home than he'd felt in years.

"You said you needed me, so I came right away." Sadie waited for him to pull back before she released her embrace. But even then, she didn't step back. She stayed close, observing him with those warm green eyes of hers.

"I hope I didn't put you in a bind," he murmured. He got creative when he stayed up late. Sadie got loopy.

"You didn't. Now, how about I come in and we have some doughnuts?"

Carter felt himself grin. Though he regretted any trouble she'd gone through to be here, he didn't regret the fact that she was here. It was great to see Sadie. In fact, he didn't realize how much he missed her until just now.

At that moment, Bo came galloping down the hall and skidded to a stop in front of her. Sadie giggled before rubbing the dog's head. "And who is this?"

"This is Bo. He's my right-hand man."

"It's so nice to meet you, Bo." She rubbed his head again, moving her hands down to his ears and then his jowls.

Bo soaked up every minute of her affection, sitting at attention with his ears perked and tail wagging.

Carter reminded himself to stop staring and nodded toward the kitchen. "Come on in. I'll get you some coffee. You must be tired."

"Coffee sounds wonderful. It was a longer trip than I thought it would be. The two ferries to get here nearly put me over the edge."

"Some people like being here for that very reason. Traveling here takes effort. Not everybody wants to make the trip—only people who really want to be here are willing to put in the effort."

"Well, you're definitely important enough to me that I wanted to put in the effort." Sadie lowered her voice, her tone letting him know she was serious. "And I can't complain about the view. The sun rose over the water as I was on the first ferry, and I've never seen anything like it. It reminded me of watermelon and mango."

"Watermelon and mango?"

"Sure. I've been pretty obsessed with those fruits ever since I went to the Caribbean."

He raised his eyebrows. "The Caribbean? I never saw you as the Caribbean type of girl."

"I'm trying to push myself out of my comfort zone." She shrugged. "What can I say?"

"Good for you." Carter figured there was a story there, but he decided to ask later. "Okay, you sit. I'll get the coffee and then we can catch up."

Sadie smiled. "I would like that. I would like it a lot."

SADIE OBSERVED Carter over a cup of coffee, trying not to make her scrutiny too obvious. His face was still thin, his build lean, and he had a sloppy yet stylish way of dressing—one that seemed popular with male musicians. His hair was messy, and his eyes were full of depth and creativity.

But there was also something different about him. Some of the sparkle had faded from his eyes. His expression almost seemed haggard.

But he was still as handsome as ever. No one could deny that.

In fact, in high school all the girls had gone crazy over him—especially when he pulled out his guitar and began to sing. He'd had no shortage of dates or groupies, even as a teenager.

Everybody had known that Carter Denver was going to be somebody, that he had star potential.

But now here he was living in a dark apartment over a fudge shop, with only his dog as a roommate.

In Sadie's gut, she sensed he wasn't happy. That he wasn't *really* happy.

And maybe that he hadn't ever gotten over what happened with Allison.

The thought made sadness press on her.

When they finished their chitchat, Sadie reached across the table and squeezed his hand. "It's really great to catch up, Carter. But I know small talk isn't what you called me for. What's going on?"

At the subject change, his gaze darkened. Whatever had happened, he didn't really want to talk about it. But he must have realized that he *needed* to talk about it. He wouldn't have called her here otherwise.

"Oh, Sadie." He pulled away from her and put both hands over his face as agony laced his features. "You're going to think I'm crazy."

"Try me. I've seen a lot of crazy. I wouldn't put you on that list. Not yet, at least."

That didn't even get a smile out of him.

This must be serious.

He lowered his hands and rested them on the table. But the look in his eyes nearly took her breath away. Whatever he was going through, it was serious and tearing him apart inside.

Sadie only hoped she had what it took to help him through this. Sure, she was a certified life coach and therapist. But that didn't give her superhero powers when it came to solving other people's problems.

If only life were that easy.

Besides, she had a secret she'd never shared with him.

She'd been in love with Carter since high school.

But after he and Allison got together, Sadie put her feelings aside. Her friendships were more important than romance. She'd stuck with that conviction until this day.

"What's going on, Carter?" she prodded softly.

His gaze met hers, and Sadie saw the pain in the depths of his eyes.

He licked his lips before finally saying, "I thought that I saw Allison yesterday while I was doing a concert."

Sadie sucked in a breath. She wanted to remain objective and level-headed.

But Carter's words took her breath away. Made her head spin. Made her worry quadruple.

"But Allison's dead, Carter," she whispered.

He squeezed his eyes shut, his features pinched with grief and confusion. "I know, Sadie. Believe me, I know."

CHAPTER FIVE

SADIE LISTENED as Carter recounted what happened. Her concern grew with every new detail.

"Carter . . ." She struggled to find the right words. "I don't know what to say."

He squeezed the skin between his eyes, a battle clearly raging inside him. "I don't either. I feel like I'm losing my mind."

She leaned closer, her heart aching with a desire to comfort him. "I'm here now. We'll figure this out. Together."

The first trace of a smile brushed his lips before disappearing. "You've always been there for me, Sadie. I can't tell you how much I appreciate that."

"Of course. That's what friends are for." Her

voice cracked as she said the words. "But do you know what I think you need now?"

He waited for her to continue.

"You need sleep also. You've had a long night, and you need to get some rest. Everything is always clearer after some shuteye."

"So do you. You drove all night—"

"I'll be fine," she insisted. "I need to get ready for my next podcast anyway. Besides, I should stay awake while you sleep, to keep an eye on you. Just in case. You know . . . head injury and everything."

He didn't say anything for a moment before finally nodding. "If you don't mind, I think I will lie down then."

As he stood, Sadie copied the action. He started toward the living room but paused. When he did, Sadie reached up and skimmed her hand across his cheek. He'd grown a beard since she'd seen him last, but it was a little too unkempt to fit him. She couldn't help but think that he also needed a haircut. Maybe even a shower.

Her heart throbbed into her ribcage.

She should have been here for him earlier. But Carter had pushed her away. Sadie figured if he needed her that he would call.

And he had.

She just worried it was too late.

"I've missed you, Carter." She pulled her hand down, realizing her touch had lingered too long.

"I've missed you too, Sadie." His eyes locked on hers as a sad smile whispered across his lips. "If it's okay, I'll lie on the couch. Seems easier that way."

"Perfect. I'll sit in the chair and work. Bo will keep me company."

She followed Carter into the living room. He nearly collapsed on the brown leather sofa. In one fluid motion, he grabbed the blanket draped over the back and pulled it over him while lying down.

Sadie leaned toward him and gave him a friendly kiss on the forehead. "Get some rest. Then we'll talk some more."

She tried to hide the concern she felt.

But what if her friend really was losing his mind?

———

AS SADIE SAT cross-legged in the oversized chair near Carter, she organized the notes for an upcoming podcast. She'd ventured into the media two years ago, and she already had five hundred thousand followers.

In fact, she'd cut back on her consulting work to

focus more on the podcast lately. Thanks to endorsement deals, she was able to make a living this way and help even more people than she had with her one-on-one coaching business.

She broadcasted twice a week and took questions from listeners who emailed them in advance. On occasion, she featured one of them on her show live. Thankfully, Sadie had pre-recorded her next four episodes so she could give all her time and attention to Carter.

She sighed and glanced over at Carter again. His chest evenly rose and fell. He was asleep.

Good. Maybe with some rest, he would find clarity.

Because there was no way he'd seen Allison last night. Her death had been conclusive. She couldn't have survived that auto accident.

With all the years that had passed, Sadie thought Carter would be over Allison by now. But apparently, he wasn't—not if he was imagining seeing Allison around town.

She frowned at the thought of it.

Sadie would stay here for as long as it took to make sure Carter was okay, she decided. She couldn't leave him at a time like this.

Besides, maybe her visit would bring the closure she needed.

She glanced around his place. It was located off the boardwalk—at the far end of the walkway, away from the busiest retail area, as far as she could tell—and it had a separate entrance from the shop below. Knick-knacks from Carter's travels decorated various surfaces —a table covering from Africa, a wooden bowl from South America, some cattle horns from out West.

The place had an artistic touch that matched Carter. He really had built a life for himself here, hadn't he?

As Sadie looked back at her notepad, a knock sounded at the door. She glanced at Carter. He still slept, his breathing still even and his eyes still closed.

Quietly, Sadie rose and hurried to the door before the sound woke him. A pretty blonde stood on the balcony-like deck stretching across the front of the building. A wrinkle formed between the woman's eyes when she spotted Sadie inside Carter's apartment.

Sadie tensed, wondering if she'd put herself in the middle of an awkward situation. Could this be Carter's girlfriend?

"Hi there," the woman started. "I'm Cassidy

Chambers. I'm the police chief here in town and a friend of Carter. I wanted to check on him after the incident last night."

Sadie released her breath as things clicked in place. She stepped outside to give Carter some more quiet.

"I'm Sadie Thompson." She held out her hand. "I'm an old friend of Carter's. He called me last night."

"I'm glad you came. He was pretty shaken up last time I saw him." Cassidy paused. "I'm guessing he told you what happened?"

Sadie nodded, interested in hearing this woman's take on last night's events. Maybe she had some insight that could assist Sadie in helping Carter.

"It sounds like the evening was pretty traumatic for him," Sadie said. "Did you catch the person who did this to him?"

"We're running prints on the crowbar, but nothing has turned up yet. Unfortunately, it happened in an alley, and no one saw anything."

Sadie pressed her lips together, hating the sound of that. "Hopefully, you'll get a lead so Carter can put this behind him."

"That's what we're hoping as well. My husband

and I consider Carter a good friend. We don't like seeing friends get hurt."

"I'm glad he's found people here he can depend on." That realization brought a small measure of comfort to Sadie. As did the smell of chocolate fudge that floated up from below. How could Carter stay skinny while smelling this all day long?

As Cassidy nodded and took a step back, Sadie glanced behind her.

Her lungs froze when she saw someone peering around a building across the boardwalk.

Someone who looked just like . . . Allison.

CHAPTER SIX

"WHAT IS IT?" Cassidy glanced behind her, her entire body ready for action.

Sadie pointed to the building across the sidewalk, still unsure if she believed her own eyes. "I thought I saw . . . Allison."

"What?" Cassidy took off in a run down the wooden steps. "Stay here. Go inside and lock the door."

At the sound of Cassidy's authoritative words, Sadie did just that. She locked the door, her heart suddenly pounding out of control as her thoughts spun.

What if Carter hadn't just been seeing things? What if there was someone on this island who really did look like Allison?

But one question disturbed her even more.

That woman had been looking right at Sadie. Whoever she was, the woman had wanted her presence to be known.

But why?

That didn't settle well with Sadie.

"What's going on?" someone grumbled behind her.

Sadie nearly jumped out of her skin. She hadn't even heard Carter get up. But suddenly, he was standing behind her with that sleepy look in his eyes.

She wanted to tell him that it was nothing. But she wouldn't lie to him. She respected him too much for that.

"This probably isn't what you're going to want to hear," Sadie started, feeling the wrinkle form between her eyes.

"What is it, Sadie?"

She swallowed hard. "I thought I just saw Allison."

His eyes widened and his grogginess disappeared faster than a one-hit wonder in Nashville. "Where?"

"I was talking to your friend Cassidy on the deck

when I thought I saw Allison peering around a building across the street."

Carter reached for the door, but Sadie pushed herself in front of it. "Cassidy went after her. She said we needed to stay here."

Carter tried to reach around her. "But I need to know—"

Sadie gently placed her hand on his chest. "Let Cassidy handle this. You're in no state to go chasing after somebody."

His haunted gaze met hers, his eyes changing from determined to grief-stricken. "What does this mean, Sadie? Could Allison have survived that car crash?"

Sadie shook her head, sticking to her guns. "I don't see how. There's just no way she could have made it."

Carter continued to stare at her, but the hope in his eyes faded as her words seemed to settle over him. "You're right. She couldn't have survived."

Did Carter still love Allison? Sadie wondered. And, if so, why did that thought cause an ache in her chest?

She had no business being disappointed. It was Carter's grief, and he was free to do with it what he wanted.

But maybe there was a part of Sadie that wished he'd moved on . . . for more than one reason.

For now, they just needed to wait and see if Cassidy found this mystery woman.

Because something very strange was going on here in Lantern Beach—something that left Sadie unsettled.

———————

CARTER WAS ETERNALLY grateful that Sadie had come to help him sort out his thoughts. His head pounded, and he had no idea what to make of everything.

But Sadie always knew how to make everything better.

It was one of her talents—putting the pieces back together. She was so good at doing it that she'd made a career of it, and she was now one of the most sought-out life coaches on the East Coast.

Normally, Carter might think being a life coach was some kind of quackery. But not knowing Sadie the way that he did. She was an amazing friend. He only wished he could say the same for himself.

He'd really dropped the ball in that area, but he hoped it wasn't too late to make things right again.

He ran a hand over his face.

Sleep had felt good. But he had been pulled out of his REM cycle when he heard the commotion at the front door. He couldn't wait to find out if Cassidy was able to catch the woman—to catch Allison.

Could it really be her? The idea seemed so outlandish. But Carter knew what he'd seen—he knew *who* he'd seen.

Finally, a knock sounded at the door. Before Sadie could stop him, he reached around her and jerked it open.

Cassidy stood there.

Alone.

Disappointment filled him at the sight.

Cassidy frowned and shook her head. "Can I come in?"

He pulled the door open wider, trying to hide his frustration. "Of course."

"I'm sorry, Carter," Cassidy said. "I went after her, but she had too much of a head start. The woman disappeared around the corner and then she was gone. I searched everywhere, but I have no idea how she gave me the slip."

"But you saw her, right?" Carter waited eagerly for Cassidy's response. Maybe he wasn't crazy. Not if other people had also seen the ghost from his past.

Cassidy paused before offering a brief head shake. "I didn't see her. But Sadie did."

He stepped back and ran a hand through his hair. He'd felt so hopeful for a moment, hopeful that he might have answers. Now he was right back where he started.

Cassidy's gaze remained on him. Carter felt it. He braced himself for whatever she had to say.

"Do you want to tell me what's going on?" she finally asked.

"Not really." Carter looked up, knowing what was coming. Knowing he couldn't keep Cassidy in the dark about this any longer. "But I will. Why don't you have a seat?"

CHAPTER SEVEN

SADIE LOWERED herself onto the couch beside Carter and prepared to offer any kind of support he might need.

Though she hadn't seen Carter in years, she knew him well enough to know that Allison wouldn't be easy for him to talk about. In fact, if she had to guess, he probably didn't talk about her at all.

Cassidy sat in the seat across from them and rubbed Bo's head. "Carter?"

He nodded, his whole body hunched forward with tension. "There's a lot you don't know about me, Cassidy. A lot I don't *want* people to know about me."

"You know we love you here, Carter." Cassidy

lowered her voice. "Whatever you need to tell me, it's okay. We all have our own pasts."

The police chief almost spoke like she personally understood. But her words were true. Sadie had learned that everyone had skeletons in their closets —some were just scarier than others.

Carter ran a hand over his mouth again.

Sadie longed to reach out to him, to try to offer him any kind of emotional support. But she couldn't share the details for him. It was his story to tell, not hers.

He glanced at Sadie, and she gave him a nod, signaling that it was okay.

"Sadie and I go way back," he started, his voice sounding thinner than usual. "The two of us met in high school. I was a bit of a loner, and Sadie was the opposite. She was friends with everybody. It seemed like she had a long line of people always wanting to get her advice and to hear some of her optimism in hopes of it rubbing off on them."

Sadie smiled. It wasn't that she was friends with everyone—it was mostly that people liked a listening ear.

"My school rezoned their districts, and all my friends ended up at a different high school. It was pretty much like starting over for me—something I was never great at."

"It's never easy," Cassidy said.

"Sadie started sitting with me at lunch and pulled me out of my shell," Carter continued. "She encouraged me with my music and helped to make me into the person that I became."

"I don't know about that . . ." Sadie knew he was giving her too much credit.

"It's true." Carter shrugged. "About a month into our friendship, Allison joined us. Allison was new at the school—she'd just moved to town and didn't know anybody. Sadie invited Allison to sit with us at lunch, and the three of us were pretty much inseparable after that."

Cassidy glanced at Sadie, as if seeing her in a new light, and nodded. "It's always great to have true friends."

"The three of us even decided to go to college together," Carter continued. "Allison and I both decided to study music, and Sadie studied psychology. Eventually, through our studies, Allison and I bonded over our love of music. We formed a duo."

"And Sadie?"

Carter glanced at her. "For a while, Sadie acted as our manager. Allison and I started doing shows locally, and then our reach expanded. It kept growing, and eventually Allison and I decided to go on the road together."

Cassidy nodded, as if absorbing every detail of the conversation. "Go on."

Carter glanced at Sadie again and let out a sigh. "With time, Allison and I started dating. We kept doing music, and a label offered us a contract."

"Were you a part of that contract?" Cassidy asked Sadie.

Sadie shook her head. "I could have gone on the road with them. But I really wanted to finish getting my degree. It was important to me."

But even as Sadie said the words, she remembered that agonizing decision. Remembered the realization that her two best friends were going on without her and she'd be left behind.

Sadie was too pragmatic to give up her career goals to follow her friends' dreams. She had dreams of her own. Besides, she'd seen the bond forming between Carter and Allison. She'd known things were changing.

It had been a hard realization to swallow. But she had no choice except to see the truth for what it was.

"Did this duo the two of you formed have a name?" Cassidy asked.

"We did," Carter said. "Sunshine and Rain."

Cassidy's lips parted in surprise, and she slowly nodded. "I remember you guys. You sang 'Dark Night Before the Dawning of Love,' right? I had no idea you were a part of that, Carter."

"Allison was always the showman of our duo," Carter said. "Or the show *woman*, I should say. She loved the spotlight. I was more of the guitar player and songwriter. She was my muse."

Something about his words made the ache in Sadie's heart pulse harder, stronger.

"Hearing your story really answers a lot of the questions I had about you," Cassidy said. "But what does that have to do with what's happening here now?"

Sadie saw the emotions rolling over Carter's features at Cassidy's question. Sadie placed a hand on his back, trying to soothe his frayed nerves and offer him silent support.

He drew in a shaky breath. "Everything didn't remain sunny all the time between Allison and me. Eventually, we had artistic differences about what direction we should go."

"Like what?" Cassidy asked.

"Allison wanted to reach for the sky until we were a household name, and I was happy to do small shows for a loyal audience. We couldn't see eye-to-eye. That affected our relationship, not just professionally but romantically. We began to fight quite a bit."

Sadie remembered those days. Carter and Allison had both called Sadie asking for advice. She hadn't wanted to take sides, so she'd tried to help both of them see different perspectives. But she wasn't sure her listening ear or advice had done any good because their conflict never resolved.

"Allison and I eventually decided to take a break." Carter's voice cracked. "Honestly, the band was on the rocks. We were in the middle of the tour, and we had some great endorsement deals. To anyone on the outside, it seemed like we were on the cusp of something great. We hadn't made it to the big time yet, but it definitely seemed like we were on our way. Our songs were moving up the charts, and our sales were growing. But working together was one of the hardest things I've ever done."

"I can imagine," Cassidy said.

"Finally, I decided to call it quits for good," Carter said. "Nothing big happened that caused me to make the decision. But I'd been thinking about it for a long time. I knew it was the right thing. So I told Allison that I couldn't do it anymore—the band or dating her. To her, it seemed sudden."

"What then?"

"I told her she could continue without me. But she said she couldn't. The fight ended with her getting mad at me and stomping out to her car so she could catch some fresh air. That's what she liked to do. Put the windows down and turn on some music and drive fast. She said it helped her clear her thoughts."

Sadie felt her stomach clench because she knew what was coming.

"After she left, she hit a tree. Died on the scene. I haven't stopped blaming myself since then."

Cassidy frowned, compassion saturating her gaze. "I'm really sorry to hear that, Carter. I had no idea."

"It's okay. I don't share about it very often."

"I guess that eventually led you to Lantern Beach?"

"A friend had a place here, and I came to visit him. Something about this island helped me feel like maybe I could heal. My friend eventually moved on, but I stayed. After a couple of years, I decided that maybe I could sing around town. I didn't need money since I'm still earning off the royalties of my songs. But I thought if I played music again, maybe I would start healing."

"Up until today, I would say that worked," Cassidy said.

"I would have said the same thing." Carter hung his head again. "I know I saw Allison. I know it sounds crazy. I know she's dead. But I saw her."

"If she's dead, then who else could this person have been?" Cassidy asked. "A tourist that maybe looked like her?"

"If you had said that to me an hour ago, that's exactly what I would have thought," Sadie said. "But I saw this woman too. She looked at me. It was almost like she wanted me to know that she was there."

Cassidy stiffened. "I don't like the sound of this."

"Neither do I," Sadie admitted. "I don't know what's going on. I just know that something isn't right here."

Cassidy let out a breath before standing, decision in her gaze. "Let me do this for you. I'll look at the security footage in the area and see if I can find anything. I'll also put in some calls to a couple of friends and see if I can find the autopsy report for Allison. That way you can know once and for all that she was really in that car and not somebody else. Maybe it will set your mind at ease."

Carter nodded, his gaze still haggard but now with a touch of hope. "It would."

"Let me help you find some answers then. I'll get started now."

"I appreciate it, Cassidy," Carter said.

"I'd want someone to do the same for me." Cassidy offered a nod at Sadie. "And if either of you need anything, let me know. I'll be around."

Sadie already liked this woman. She seemed smart and tough.

And maybe she really could help them find answers. That's what Sadie prayed, at least.

CHAPTER EIGHT

AS SOON AS CASSIDY LEFT, Carter turned toward Sadie. "Have I told you how glad I am that you came?"

A slow grin spread across her face. "You did mention that."

"Really. I feel like I'm losing my mind right now."

Her grin disappeared and she reached for him, resting her hand on his knee. "But you're not. I saw this woman too."

"You don't know how much better that makes me feel to know that someone like you saw her as well."

"Someone like me?" She raised her eyebrows as if unsure how to take his words.

Carter shrugged. "I'm a musician. I'm given to flights of fancy and creative bursts. But you . . . you're levelheaded and logical. You don't make up stories or imagine things that aren't there. If someone like you thinks you saw Allison, then maybe I'm not crazy after all."

Sadie's hand tightened on his knee. "I don't think you're crazy, Carter."

Their gazes caught, and Carter felt something lurch inside him.

What *was* that? He knew. A certain peace washed over him at Sadie's acceptance.

Sadie had always made him feel that way, ever since the first moment they'd met. Having Sadie believe in him had changed Carter's entire life. He hadn't been exaggerating when he'd told Cassidy that.

"Look, why don't we go get something to eat?" he suggested. "Maybe it would be good to get out of here."

Another part of him hoped that he might see Allison again. He'd never find answers just staying inside.

"You don't have anything to make here? I could cook ..."

He shrugged. "You know me. I've never been much on cooking—not when I can go out to eat."

Sadie let out a quick chuckle. "That was always

you. I can't deny that. Steak n' Shake practically reserved us both an honorary booth when we were in college."

"And their hamburgers will always hold a special place in my heart."

"As they should."

"So what do you say? There's this place called The Crazy Chefette that has some great lunch specials." He glanced at his watch and saw that he'd slept nearly four hours. "We can probably catch the end of them."

Sadie nodded. "That sounds good. Let's go get some lunch and catch up a little more."

"First, how about if I grab a quick shower?"

"I think that's a great idea." She reached up and touched his beard. "And maybe trim that up a bit while you're at it?"

He let out a chuckle. "I make no promises. I'll be back in a few."

He disappeared down the hall, feeling a surprising spring in his step.

AS SADIE'S and Carter's chuckles faded, Sadie took another sip of her jalapeño-infused lemonade—a restaurant special.

Lunch had been great. She and Carter had reminisced over better times as they'd eaten some crab cheesecake at The Crazy Chefette. Apparently, the restaurant was known for its unique flavor combinations—and her lunch had proven it.

Though the name of the dish hadn't been appealing, the cheesy crab dip with crusty bread slices had been delicious.

Mostly, Sadie had enjoyed the company.

Carter was a great storyteller. He didn't let a lot of people into his circle, but once someone earned a spot, they were a friend for life.

Maybe that was why everyone was shocked when he'd broken up with Allison. He was the loyal type, the kind who didn't give up on people. But he'd made that tough choice.

Sadie couldn't blame him. Allison had let their success go to her head. She hadn't been the same person Carter had fallen in love with. She was so hungry for fame that she'd lost sight of what was important.

It happened all too often in the music industry. Sadie had seen it with some of her clients. It was as if once they got a taste of being famous, they were hooked like a heroin addict after their first hit.

Sadie saw Carter scan the restaurant again.

He was looking around for her, Sadie realized. He was waiting for Allison to show up.

Her stomach clenched at the realization.

Sadie needed to remind Carter that, whoever that woman was, she'd hit him over the head with a crowbar earlier.

Instead of finding her, maybe he should be more interested in never seeing her again.

But Sadie didn't tell him that. Not now, at least. Why ruin an otherwise pleasant moment?

"Maybe we should get back," Carter suggested.

"I guess. There are a lot of people waiting to find a table, and we don't want to take up too much valuable real estate."

"I guess we don't." Carter rose and pulled out his wallet. Before Sadie could stop him, he dropped some cash on the table. "This is on me. It's the least that I can do since you came all this way."

"You don't have to."

"But I want to. Come on." Carter offered his arm to her, and Sadie slipped her hand into the crook of it.

The two of them had always been affectionate with each other. Physical touch was Sadie's love language, so she had a tendency to crave hugs and pats on the back. Plus, something about being affectionate with Carter seemed so natural, like it shouldn't be any other way.

Sadie mentally chided herself at the thought. She couldn't think like that. The two were just friends.

So why was it that every guy she'd ever dated had never measured up?

She asked herself that question a lot, but still hadn't found an answer that she was willing to accept.

The two of them stepped outside and into the sunshine. With Sadie's arm still in his, they started back to his place.

They'd walked to The Crazy Chefette. Why not? Right now, it was a beautiful day outside and stretching their legs had felt good. Later today, a storm system was forecast to come through the area.

But when Sadie got back to Carter's apartment, she hoped to take a nap. Her long drive was finally catching up with her. For now, she would enjoy being outside and smelling the salty ocean air.

As they strolled, Carter pointed out various businesses and regaled her with stories of all the happenings on the island. If he hadn't insisted his stories were true, Sadie might not believe him.

Zombie-like drug addicts had invaded the island? A cult had taken up residence at an old campground? The whole place had gone dark because of a terrorist attack? Those things seemed larger than life for such a peaceful island.

They walked along the sidewalk, enjoying the temperate autumn air. The sky glowered above them, promising rain soon. Even the breeze seemed to whisper about what was coming.

But right now, the air felt fresh and Sadie's lungs loosened for a moment.

The sound of a car accelerating drew her attention away from the cresting sand dunes in the distance.

A red Mustang came toward them.

A red Mustang?

Allison had driven a red Mustang.

The pulsing of Sadie's heart turned into a dull thud in her ears.

In fact, that was the vehicle Allison had been driving when she died.

Sadie felt Carter's muscles tighten beneath her hand.

The next instant, the car accelerated again.

The vehicle swerved toward the sidewalk . . . headed right toward Carter and Sadie.

CHAPTER NINE

"SADIE!" Carter yelled.

He reached for her, knowing he had to get her out of the way. But just as he grabbed her arms, the car clipped her side.

Sadie cried out and fell to the ground.

Carter sank down beside her, searching for any injuries. She appeared fine.

His gaze wandered up quickly, trying to memorize the license plate. But mud covered the numbers and letters. Carter couldn't make any of them out.

"Are you okay?" He stared into Sadie's eyes, as worry pulsed through him.

She glanced down at herself, as if unsure how to answer. No doubt shock was setting in. "I'm fine . . . I think."

"Does anything feel broken? I can take you to the clinic. I can—"

She raised her hand. "No, I'm fine. Really. Just shaken. Maybe a little bruised."

He glanced down the street again and frowned. "That driver was aiming for us."

His words sounded grim—sickeningly so. Just what was going on here? Why was someone targeting them? It made no sense.

"If you hadn't grabbed me when you did, that driver might have really run me over instead of just clipping me." Sadie drew in a shaky breath, still looking dazed.

Carter swallowed hard. Hearing the words out loud only made the sick feeling in his stomach grow. "I know."

Sadie's gaze met his. "That looked like Allison's car."

"It did."

"Were you able to see who was driving?"

He shook his head. "Unfortunately, the windows were tinted."

Sadie frowned. "That's what I thought too. But . . . the driver almost looked like . . . a blonde."

Carter licked his lips. "I know."

Sadie had seen Allison. Seen the car. Been on the other end of this vengeance.

The thought no longer comforted him, though.

Sadie rubbed her elbow, her face scrunched in distress. "I don't know what's going on here, Carter. But I don't like it."

ALTHOUGH SADIE WANTED to go back to Carter's apartment to unwind, the police showed up a few minutes after the accident. Someone must have seen what happened and reported it.

Specifically, Cassidy showed up. After looking Sadie over, the police chief escorted the two of them to the station to get their statements. After Sadie and Carter told her what happened, she frowned and turned a computer screen toward them.

"As I was investigating earlier, I found one business nearby with a video camera," she started. "I got the footage and reviewed it."

"And?" Carter's voice rose.

Cassidy hit a key on her computer. "This is what came up."

Sadie leaned closer. The footage appeared grainy and not the best quality. But she saw the front of a building—a candy store. The angle of the lens stretched from the front door of the shop to the start of the alley running beside it.

Cassidy fast-forwarded before slowing down. "Here."

Sadie studied the screen, her lungs frozen with anticipation.

She sucked in a breath at what she saw.

A woman with blonde hair crouched near the corner.

A woman who looked exactly like Allison.

She and Carter exchanged a glance.

What if Allison hadn't died that night?

Maybe that was a question they truly needed to examine.

CHAPTER TEN

CARTER LEANED BACK in his chair in Cassidy's office, dumbfounded at what he'd seen.

The woman on the screen hadn't even gone into that candy shop. She'd simply been peering around the corner, most likely looking for Carter.

She'd been hoping he would see her.

But why would Allison do that?

And was this person even Allison? The woman certainly looked like her. Dressed like her. Fixed her hair like her. Even had the same pert nose as she did.

A bad feeling brewed in his gut, and his head began pounding. Until he made sense of things, that thrumming headache would remain.

"I'm going to have my officers keep their eyes open for this woman," Cassidy said. "There's a warrant out for her arrest, especially now that she's a suspect in a hit-and-run. We'll also be looking for that red Mustang. It should be easy to spot."

"Are you able to canvas the whole island?" Sadie asked, still rubbing her elbow.

Carter prayed she wasn't badly hurt, but she'd refused to go to the clinic. He had no room to talk since he hadn't gone last night either. But he'd feel better if he knew Sadie truly was okay—especially since this was all his fault.

"We are." Cassidy glanced at a map of the long, narrow island that hung on the wall beside them. "We'll make our way down each of the streets to see if we find the vehicle. That's not to say that we're definitely going to come across it. Criminals are creative. We once had someone hide their car in a marsh. Then they couldn't get it out. There are some interesting people out there for sure."

Any other time, Carter might enjoy hearing some of Cassidy's stories. But not now. Not when there was so much on the line.

"Thank you for everything you're doing," Carter said.

Cassidy's wry smile slipped into a frown. "Of course. I want you to stay safe. Whatever is going on here, this woman is dangerous. I suggest the two of you remain inside tonight. I'll make sure an officer goes past your apartment every ten minutes or so to keep an eye on things."

"Thank you." Sadie leaned forward, her gaze latched onto Cassidy's. "That makes me feel a little better. It's good to know you're taking this seriously."

A few minutes later, Carter and Sadie were escorted back to Carter's place by Officer Dillinger. The two of them said very little on the short drive. Instead, the officer talked about his new baby girl. It was actually sweet to hear how smitten the man was with his daughter.

Carter hoped that one day he would have a family of his own. That possibility often felt very far away—if not impossible. He had to get rid of some ghosts from his past first, and he wasn't sure that would ever happen.

As soon as Carter and Sadie stepped into his apartment, Carter turned to her. They both needed something to distract them.

There was only one thing he could think of.

"What do you say we have one of our old movie marathons?" he suggested. "It's been a long time, but it could be fun."

They had an eclectic list of favorites. *Jurassic Park. Dumb and Dumber. The Princess Bride. Jaws—*

just to name a few. The two of them used to have at least one movie night a month together. The routine helped them both unwind. Allison had usually chosen to go partying instead.

"That sounds like the perfect way to spend the rest of the day," Sadie said. "I'll make the popcorn. But we should start now. Because I have a feeling I'm going to turn in early tonight."

"No problem. Let's get started."

"OH MY GOODNESS, Emily totally had a crush on you." Sadie laughed.

Even though *Grease* played in the background, she and Carter had barely watched any of the old movie. Instead, they reminisced about better times.

Sometimes, Sadie would give anything to go back to those days. Other times, she wouldn't touch her teenage years with a ten-foot pole.

"Emily did *not* like me." Carter shook his head, light from the TV screen illuminating his face. "She had a crush on every boy in the school."

"She wrote 'Emily Hearts Carter' all over her notebooks. I sat beside her in calculus. Believe me. I saw it all. In fact, all the girls used to come to me and want me to put in a good word with you. You remember Melinda Jenkins?"

He let out a groan. "That girl made me nervous. She cornered me in a locker room one time, and I thought she was going to force me to make out with her."

Sadie let out a laugh. "I think that was her plan all along. I'm telling you, there's something about you that makes girls swoon. Maybe that's what made you so good at what you did. You had talent plus charisma plus kindness. Win, win, win!"

His smile faded. "Allison was the one with the charisma."

"I beg to differ." Sadie's voice caught, and she told herself not to say too much. Otherwise, she might give away how she felt. Nor did she want to talk poorly of the dead.

The most-likely dead.

She frowned.

"You're talking like I was the one who got all the attention," Carter said. "But you would sit there and be so nice to everybody in school. Half the boys in our class had a crush on you because they took your kindness as a sign that you liked them."

Sadie shook her head. "I don't know about . . ."

"I do. You had guys following you around like

poor little puppy dogs. You were just clueless. I mean, didn't four different guys ask you to the prom?"

She shrugged. "Maybe."

She'd secretly wanted to go with Carter. Instead, she and Carter had decided to each go solo. At the last minute, Allison's date had canceled on her, and she'd begged Carter to go with her instead.

"Finally, all those boys got the hint and went on their merry little ways," Carter said. "And you were none the wiser about what a hot commodity you were."

Sadie rolled her eyes. "That is not true. Allison was the one with all the guys liking her."

"She was definitely a flirt."

"And gorgeous," Sadie reminded him.

Carter shrugged, some of the lightheartedness disappearing from his gaze. "Maybe we shouldn't talk about her right now. It was nice talking about other things, wasn't it?"

Sadie picked up a piece of popcorn from the bowl and started to bring it to her mouth. "It was."

Instead of eating the kernel, she tossed it at Carter. His eyes widened in surprise before he let out a long chuckle.

"Oh no, you didn't . . ." he muttered.

Sadie grinned. "Oh, yes, I did."

He took a handful of popcorn and started throwing pieces at her like missiles.

She giggled and threw them right back.

In an instant, it was like they'd picked up right where they left off so long ago. Fun. Playful. Friendly.

It certainly didn't feel like six years had passed without them really talking.

Sadie had missed this. She had missed how easy things were between them. That didn't come along every day.

Maybe the fact that Carter thought he'd seen Allison was a blessing in disguise. It had brought the two of them together again.

"You've got a popcorn kernel in your hair." Carter reached forward and plucked it out before showing it to Sadie.

As he did, their gazes caught.

Sadie froze. Did he feel what she did? Or was she just trying to live out some kind of teenage fantasy?

Carter was right about one thing. Sadie had always been a bit clueless when it came to men. Even though she could give advice to the best of them, when it came to her own love life she had no idea what she was doing.

Even right now.

Especially right now.

Carter's gaze mesmerized her as they stared at each other. Sadie opened her mouth, trying to think of something witty to say to deflect the moment.

Instead, her gaze flicked behind Carter to the window.

A shadow moved there.

Any romantic thoughts left her mind.

Instead, Sadie grabbed Carter's arm and pointed to the window. "Carter, someone's outside."

CHAPTER ELEVEN

CARTER STOOD and pushed Sadie behind him. "Maybe we should call Cassidy."

"Probably."

Instead of doing that, Carter crept closer to the window. He was more of a lover than a fighter. Hand-to-hand combat had never been his thing.

But if Allison was outside his apartment, he wanted to see her. To talk to her. To demand answers.

Then he remembered that this woman had hit him over the head and knocked him out. That she'd tried to run them over.

This wasn't anyone to be messed with.

If this *was* Allison, she'd changed. The Allison

whom Carter had known was a bit wild but never unstable. Not like this.

Sadie grabbed his arm, halting him mid-step. "I don't think you should go out there, Carter."

She was probably right. But he couldn't stop moving forward. His need to know superseded his common sense.

"Carter." Sadie's voice cracked as she tugged his arm, begging him to stay put.

He snapped back to reality.

There she was. Sadie. His voice of reason.

Carter needed her in his life. He'd always known that. When she had decided to stay at college instead of going on the road as their manager, he hadn't slept for two weeks. That's how lost he had felt without her. The emptiness had stayed with him throughout the years.

Sadie put a phone to her ear. "I'm calling the cops. You're not going out there."

He stopped where he was, disappointment biting deep. His instinct still cried out for answers.

But Sadie was right. They didn't know what they would find on the other side of that door. There was a chance that whoever it was, Sadie could be in danger also.

Carter couldn't put her through that.

So he would wait.

But that was the last thing he wanted to do.

TEN MINUTES LATER, Officer Dillinger had shown up. Cassidy was at another call and couldn't come herself.

Sadie and Carter stood in front of Carter's apartment, staring at words that had been smeared on his window in what appeared to be red lipstick.

I can't take my eyes off you.

The words were more than a phrase. They were the title of a song Carter and Allison had performed together. In fact, that tune had been one of their most popular ones.

Seeing the words in this context made Sadie's gut roil.

"Did you see anyone when you got here?" Carter asked Officer Dillinger.

The officer shook his head. "I'm sorry. I didn't. There wasn't anybody on the street when I pulled up."

Carter glanced at Sadie. "She must have written this and run, not wanting to get caught."

Sadie wore a pinched expression. "If she doesn't

want to get caught, why does she keep coming back?"

Her question hung in the air.

Carter frowned. "That's a great question. I wish I knew the answer."

"I'll take some pictures of this and file a report," Officer Dillinger said. "We've been on the lookout all day for this woman and her red Mustang, but so far we haven't found either."

Disappointment pressed deep into Sadie.

Why would someone do this? No matter how she looked at it, these offenses just didn't make any sense —and part of her job involved making sense of people's emotional messes. These events left her perplexed.

With a final nod, Officer Dillinger dismissed them to go back into the apartment.

Sadie should feel better. But she didn't.

It wasn't that she didn't trust the officer. She just knew without a doubt that the person behind these crimes was somehow off her rocker. It was the only reason someone would go to such extremes.

But just how far would this person take things? Who would have to get hurt before this madwoman stopped her rampage?

Sadie didn't like the fact that she had to ask herself that question. But she'd be unwise if she didn't.

CHAPTER TWELVE

WHEN CARTER TURNED toward Sadie after Officer Dillinger left, he saw something change in her gaze. The lighthearted fun they'd had earlier was now gone. The day had unmistakably taken a turn for the worse.

But he also saw the exhaustion capturing her features.

"You should get some sleep," he said, even as the sounds of "We Go Together" played happily in the background. "I have two extra bedrooms. You're welcome to use one."

"Now that you mention it, I am tired." Sadie nodded, almost a little too quickly. "Maybe some sleep would be a good thing."

Carter nodded and rubbed her arm. She always looked out for everyone. But who looked out for her?

He used to claim that was his job. But Carter had seriously dropped the ball.

He intended on changing that.

"You've had a long day," he reminded her.

Sadie's concerned gaze stared back at him. "So have you."

He shrugged, suddenly not caring about his own exhaustion or confusion—only Sadie's. "I can take care of myself."

She tilted her head, that deep, probing look returning to her gaze. "Can you?"

That was Sadie. Always cutting to the heart of the matter. Always making people examine the ideas they'd chosen to believe. All in an effort to help people live their best lives.

The truth was, Carter *was* exhausted. But he couldn't see himself falling asleep, not with everything that had gone on. What if that woman—possibly Allison—returned? What if she was more extreme this time?

Somebody needed to keep an eye on this place. Though an officer was driving past every ten minutes, that didn't mean something else couldn't happen. The message left on his window was proof of that.

"I'll go lie down." Carter made sure not to promise to actually go to sleep.

After another moment of studying him, Sadie finally nodded. "Okay then. We can talk more tomorrow and see if we can figure this out."

"That sounds great." But for some reason, Carter's throat burned as he said the words.

What was it about the way Sadie looked at him right now that did something strange inside him?

Maybe it was the darkness around him. Maybe it was because she was so familiar and warm. Maybe it was the fact that Carter was tired.

But all he really wanted to do was pull Sadie into his arms and give her a big hug and kiss—

No, not a kiss. Just a warm, friendly hug.

Because that's what he and Sadie were.

Friends.

Other than Allison, no one had ever known Carter as well as Sadie.

For that matter, maybe Sadie knew him even better than Allison had. He'd loved Allison, but Allison liked to make everything about her while Sadie liked to make everything about other people.

Sadie pushed one of her long, wavy strands of

hair behind her ear and offered a full smile. "Good night, Carter."

"Good night," he mumbled.

For the first time in a long time, Carter couldn't deny the fact that he was excited to see what tomorrow held. He realized he sounded crazy in light of everything that had happened.

But the excitement wasn't because of Allison—or the supposed Allison who was out there.

Carter's excitement was because tomorrow he would get to spend more time with Sadie.

AS SADIE LAY in Carter's guest bedroom, she couldn't help but notice Carter's scent on the sheets.

Did he lie in here to find inspiration for his songs? A slightly piney scent drifted from the pillow.

She lay on her back and stared at the ceiling. Even though she was tired, sleep would be hard to find tonight after everything that happened.

And, by everything that happened, she wasn't just talking about Allison.

Sadie thought she'd put her feelings for Carter behind her. But seeing him again had stirred up dormant emotions in her heart.

Her mind drifted back in time.

When Allison and Carter went on tour without her, part of Sadie had been relieved. Their departure had made things easier for her. She loved both her friends, but seeing the two of them together had been so hard. Her heart had panged with jealousy— a jealousy she hadn't wanted or fed. But, nonetheless, the emotion was still there.

Distance seemed the only way to conquer the emotion. And it had helped—some. But not completely. Her career hadn't filled the emptiness that was left without her friends, nor had new relationships or trips across the world.

There were some kinds of grief that could never be filled. There were some friendships that could never be replaced.

The message written on Carter's window floated back into her mind. *I can't take my eyes off you.*

Sadie remembered when Carter had written that song.

He and Sadie had been hanging out at a park near their college campus. The sun had been setting, and beautiful hues of orange and yellow had filled the nighttime sky. Carter had asked Sadie to meet him there.

He and Allison hadn't been dating yet, but Sadie

had suspected Carter might like Allison and that Allison might like him. Sadie still held out some kind of hope that she and Carter might eventually take their relationship to the next level.

Maybe that's what Carter had wanted to tell her, that's what the urgency was about.

After Sadie arrived, Carter had told her that he wanted to play a new song he'd written. When Sadie heard the lyrics . . . her whole world had gone still.

Had he written those lyrics for her?

After the song finished, Sadie felt speechless . . . and hopeful.

She'd waited, expecting Carter to proclaim his love, anticipating a shift in their relationship.

Instead, he'd asked, "What do you think Allison will think about it?"

Sadie's heart, once filled with excitement, had crashed into a million pieces. Somehow, she managed to pull herself together. She was nearly certain that Carter had no clue about her feelings—and she wanted to keep it that way.

Though she'd choked the words out, she'd told Carter that Allison would love it.

That was the moment Sadie knew everything was going to change.

And it did.

Now here she was, comforting Carter as Allison's ghost seemed to haunt him. Even in her death, she was still here, still between them.

Would this issue with someone who looked like Allison resolve? When it did, would Sadie return to her life in Nashville and act like none of this had happened?

She didn't know.

Part of her wanted to do just that. The other part wanted to be bold. So what if she put her fifteen-year friendship on the line? She and Carter hadn't spoken to each other in six years anyway.

Sadie turned over in bed. She wouldn't make any snap decisions. She needed to weigh the rewards and consequences first.

Right now, she should get some rest. It was the best thing that she could do for herself—especially if she didn't want to do something she regretted.

CHAPTER THIRTEEN

DESPITE THE POUNDING RAIN OUTSIDE—
WHICH usually lured him to sleep—Carter had hardly rested all night. Instead, he'd stayed awake, listening for the sounds of anybody lurking in the shadows.

He'd heard nothing but the torrential downpour beating against his roof.

After lying in bed for a while, he'd pulled out an old box of photos.

He reminisced as he looked through the images of him and Allison smiling beside each other. There were uncountable pictures of them together—on stage, on their album cover, at award ceremonies.

Carter supposed when the two of them had named their duo Sunshine and Rain that Allison had been the sunshine and he'd been the rain. Not that he was a total Eeyore. But he'd been the more melancholy of the two, while Allison had been the extroverted Tigger.

Things had felt so perfect between them at first.

Until everything started to fall apart.

He'd learned that it was one thing to have fun together. But it was an entirely different story to work together all the time without much separation.

Being on the road and forced to make business decisions together had definitely taken its toll on their relationship. Carter had known that, at their core, he and Allison were mismatched.

Even though opposites could balance each other out, there were some opposites that would just never mix. Carter had thought music could conquer their differences, but it hadn't happened. In fact, their music had ultimately deepened the divide between them until it was impassable.

Finally, as the sun was rising, Carter climbed out of bed to get ready for the day. Then he padded into the kitchen and started the coffee.

There was no sign of Sadie. She'd always been an early riser, so either she'd changed and was no longer a morning person or she really had been bone-tired and slept in.

Carter glanced around his living room, making sure nothing was out of place. "Everything looks good, right, Bo?"

His dog sat at attention beside him. Carter reached into his treat jar and pulled out a Milk-Bone for the canine.

Despite the normal moment, Carter couldn't get the message that had been written on his window out of his mind. *I can't take my eyes off you.*

No doubt this person was trying to remind him of that song. But there was also another message there too. This person wanted to let Carter know that she was watching him.

Just what was this woman's end goal?

He let out a sigh and glanced at Bo again. "I've got to do something before my thoughts drive me mad."

Bo let out a little bark, his eyes going to the treat jar again.

Carter shook his head. "Not now, my friend. Not now."

Bo released a long breath and lay on the kitchen floor, almost as if resigned.

Maybe Carter would cook breakfast.

A smile tugged at his lips at the thought. He hadn't cooked for anyone in a long time. There were very few meals that he could put together. But he *could* make a mean omelet.

Sadie used to love his omelet with tomatoes, onions, and cheese . . . it had been her favorite.

The thought of making Sadie happy made Carter decidedly happy as well.

With that realization, he pulled out the ingredients and got busy.

SADIE PAUSED as she walked into the kitchen. She'd thought she smelled something savory and delicious wafting down the hall as she dressed.

She watched as Carter leaned over a griddle, steam rising from the surface as he hummed to himself.

Seeing him cooking at the kitchen counter caused her heart to pitter-patter in her chest. He wore a black T-shirt that showed his lean, strong physique and jeans that were just tight enough. His brown hair was still tousled with sleep.

He hadn't heard Sadie yet—the sound of pounding rain concealed her footsteps. She seized the opportunity to soak him in for another moment.

No wonder so many women had swooned over

him. What was there not to like about Carter? He was humble, kind, talented. He was sensitive, sweet, but manly.

He was basically the perfect man. In Sadie's estimation, at least.

Allison hadn't deserved him.

She sucked in a breath at the thought. Sadie had never voiced that thought aloud—and she never would. Allison had been her friend. But Allison had also been selfish, looking after no one but herself.

Carter had deserved better. He *still* deserved better than this mess he was in now.

As Bo walked over to greet her, Carter glanced over his shoulder and smiled. "Sadie! I didn't even hear you come in. Good morning."

Sadie's heart pounded into her chest. "Morning."

"I thought you might want some breakfast. Coffee is ready for you." He nodded toward the coffeepot on the other side of the kitchen.

As Sadie went to grab a cup, she glanced at him again, not bothering to hide her scrutiny. Now that she was closer, she noticed that something about Carter looked different this morning.

"You trimmed your beard," she finally murmured.

He rubbed his jaw. "I decided it was a good idea.

I've never been the scraggly sort. I think clean-cut fits me more."

"I agree. You look nice."

"Thanks." He turned back to the griddle.

Was it just Sadie's imagination or did his cheeks redden just a tinge at her words? It was probably her imagination.

She grabbed some coffee and sat at the breakfast bar to watch Carter work. As she did, she rubbed Bo's head and murmured to him about what a good boy he was.

It was good to see that everything looked normal. She assumed that meant that nothing else happened last night. Maybe they would hear an update on the investigation later today.

With any luck, maybe Cassidy had gotten a hit on some more video footage or found a witness or tracked down this woman's car. Maybe she'd heard back from her medical examiner friend who'd put in a call about Allison's accident.

Sadie just hoped that some progress was made. Because she wasn't sure how many more days like yesterday Carter could handle. She couldn't blame him. The series of events that had played out was a lot for anybody to take in.

A moment later, Carter set the plate in front of her with a flourish. "Breakfast is served."

"It's my favorite." Her mouth salivated as she looked at the omelet.

"I know." He flashed a satisfied smile.

Sadie's cheeks heated. She hadn't expected him to remember how much she loved this dish. There was something about the way Carter cooked it that she'd never been able to replicate.

She said a silent prayer before digging in. The omelet was just as good as she remembered.

Carter sat across from her with his own omelet and smiled. "Did you sleep okay?"

"As well as to be expected. You?"

He shrugged. "Can't complain."

Sadie knew what that meant. He hadn't slept. Some of his best work was done during the nighttime hours. He'd always been like that. A night owl. An insomniac.

"No updates, I'm guessing?" Sadie hated to ruin their otherwise lighthearted moment, but the question needed to be asked.

"I haven't heard anything."

"I was thinking last night as I was trying to sleep." Sadie cut the omelet with the edge of her fork and stabbed a piece. "Has there been anyone at your concerts here who made you uneasy?"

He thought about it a minute. "I don't want to point the finger at anyone—"

"Don't consider it pointed. Consider this a casual conversation."

He shrugged. "There are a couple of women here in town who come to all my shows. I know one of them liked me."

"What's her name?"

"Jessica Perkins," he said.

"And what happened with Jessica Perkins?"

He shrugged again. "Nothing. She asked me out. I told her I wasn't interested in dating anyone. End of story."

Sadie wasn't so sure that was the end of the story —at least not for Jessica.

"Besides, Jessica looks nothing like Allison."

That might be true, but Sadie stored the woman's name away in the back of her mind anyway.

"Okay, what about fan mail? Do you still get any?"

"Fan mail?" He raised his eyebrows.

"I'm assuming people send you letters still— maybe not physical letters. But emails or messages through your website. I know it's still up on the internet."

He raised his eyebrows higher. "Have you been checking me out?"

Sadie's cheeks warmed again. She'd been caught. "I decided to look it up not too long ago. I saw that the site was still there. No big deal—just curiosity."

"We still have some album sales. It's mostly digital now, which is nice because there's no real paperwork. I figured I should keep the site up, to somehow try to honor Allison's memory."

Carter had always been such a thoughtful guy. It seemed so rare, at least in Sadie's world.

Sadie pointed her fork, still laden with her omelet, at Carter. "But what about that fan mail?"

His eyes traveled back and forth as if he was trying to think of anything specific.

Then they widened.

He'd remembered something.

Sadie braced herself for whatever he was about to say.

CHAPTER FOURTEEN

"SOMEONE WHO GOES by Obsession409 has sent me probably twenty emails over the past few months." Carter retrieved his laptop and turned his computer screen so Sadie could see the messages. He'd saved them all out of an abundance of caution.

Sadie frowned. "Her name alone doesn't give me warm, fuzzy feelings."

Carter raised his eyebrows in agreement. "Me either. But this kind of thing comes with the territory when you're a musician. Some people get a little crazy about anyone in the spotlight."

Sadie scanned the text before shaking her head. "Is this Obsession409 somebody who's a fan of your old music or someone who's a current fan of what you're doing?"

"I imagine it's someone who likes the old music. As you know, I went back to my given name after everything that happened with Allison. Most people don't make the connection."

Carter Denver was his given name, but when he'd gone on the road with Allison, Allison had thought they should change their names into something more fameworthy. He'd officially become Carter Hetfield and Allison went by Allie Fairway.

Sadie studied the messages again, tapping her finger against her lips. "So, even if this lady who's sending you these messages was a fan of your music, it would be very difficult to track you down here in Lantern Beach with a different name, right?"

"I'd think so." Carter shrugged. "But technology is pretty amazing. If somebody wanted to, I bet they could figure out who I really was and find me. I mean, Allison and I talked onstage about being friends since high school. About how we grew up in Indiana together. I bet somebody could put the pieces together and figure it all out."

Sadie sucked on her bottom lip as if still processing everything. Finally, she nodded. "I bet you're right. Unfortunately. Have you tried to do any research on this Obsession lady?"

"That's not in my skill set." Carter shook his

head, now realizing that it would have been a good idea. "I *did* click on her name to see if I could find out anything else about her. But this is simply the name she used in the comment section on my website. People can write in whatever name they want. They don't have to give any other information either. My guess is that it would be nearly impossible to track her down. Besides, it's not like she's threatened me directly. It's just like her name says—she simply seems obsessed."

"I'd say," Sadie muttered. "She can quote the lyrics to your songs. Says she dreams about you day and night. She falls asleep holding a picture of you." Sadie looked up at Carter and partly rolled her eyes, partly squirmed. "That's unnerving, to say the least."

"I suppose it is." He'd felt entirely safe here up until the day before yesterday.

"Is she the only one who's sent messages like this?"

Carter pulled his laptop toward him and clicked on a few other messages. "There's some other fan mail, but nothing that really raised any red flags. You're welcome to read them. Maybe you'll see something in a different light than I did."

Sadie continued to nibble on her bottom lip, her gaze deep with thought. "What about your shows here? Have you ever had anyone who's attending get aggressive or pushy?"

Carter leaned back, trying to go back in time. He didn't usually take notes about things like this. Maybe he should have.

He sat up straighter as a memory hit him. "I *did* do a show this summer on the boardwalk as a part of a summer concert series. I was able to open for Bree Jordan."

"Bree Jordan? The pop star? That's exciting."

He shrugged. "I was hesitant to accept the gig. I didn't want to bring too much attention to myself. But in the entertainment industry, five years out of the spotlight is like a lifetime."

"What do you mean?"

"People move on to other artists who are still keeping themselves relevant. Most people's memories are short. Anyway, I opened for Bree. Afterward, this woman somehow managed to sneak backstage and corner me. She said I was the best singer she'd ever heard. Something in her eyes didn't look quite stable to me."

"And?"

Carter shrugged. "Thankfully, I had a couple of pals with me who were former Navy SEALS."

"You're hanging out with Navy SEALS?" Sadie made a face, as if trying to put those pieces together.

"It's a long story, but one of them is dating Bree. Anyway, they kind of stepped in and made an excuse about me having to be somewhere. That ended that conversation."

"And did you ever see this woman again?"

"Once when I was out at my friend's vegetable stand. Actually, I saw this woman coming and knew I couldn't stick around. I told the owner of the stand to put the items on my tab and quickly got out of there."

"Did this woman look anything like Allison?"

Carter shrugged. "She had dark hair. Maybe she was the same size. It's really hard to know. I wasn't taking notes."

In retrospect, he should have.

Sadie nodded, that contemplative look still on her face. "We'll get to the bottom of this, Carter. We just need a little more time."

He was thankful for her determination.

And he hoped she was right.

AFTER BREAKFAST, Carter and Sadie called Cassidy to see if there were any updates. The police chief told them she was still waiting to hear back from her friend with the medical examiner's office. She'd also had no luck locating the car or the woman who had been seen in that security video.

Cassidy assured them that she was still looking. They'd mentioned Jessica, just in case the woman was relevant. Cassidy said she thought Jessica was out of town, but she would look into it.

After they ended the call, Sadie and Carter cleaned up the kitchen together. Carter turned on some music, and "I Can See Clearly Now" blared through the room. They sang together as they worked, Carter totally on pitch and Sadie totally not on pitch.

Neither of them cared.

When they'd dried the last dish and put it away, they paused in front of each other in the middle of the kitchen. A moment passed between them as they stared at each other, something shifting.

Was this . . . awkwardness? Things *never* felt awkward between them. So what had changed?

Sadie would have to think about that later.

"So, since you're here . . . maybe I should show

you around the island," Carter suggested. "It's not raining as hard right now."

That sounded like a fantastic idea. Except . . . "In normal circumstances, I would love that. But given everything that's happened, I'm not sure it's safe."

He shrugged. "I thought about that. But I also know that we can't hide forever."

Sadie nodded slowly, knowing his words were true. What if this went on for weeks? Maybe hiding wasn't the solution they were looking for.

"You're right," Sadie said. "I suppose as long as we remain on guard, we should be okay, right?"

"I would think so. We just need to be smart about it." He studied her face another moment. "Lantern Beach is a great place, Sadie. I think you'd really love it here. Then again, I guess you love it in Nashville since that's where you ended up staying."

"Nashville is a great town. No one can deny that. A lot of my clients are there. Then again, now that my podcast has become popular, I've been doing a lot of things virtually and online."

Carter softly squeezed her bicep. "I'm so proud of you, Sadie. I've always admired how much you like to look out for other people."

She willed her cheeks not to heat at his touch. "If

I can help others have a little more peace in their lives, then I should."

A soft grin spread across his face. "You've always been pretty much perfect."

Carter's words made Sadie pause. "I'm far from perfect. Believe me."

He tilted his head. "Prove it."

Sadie let out a strangled laugh. "How am I supposed to do that?"

He crossed his arms, not bothering to hide the challenge in his voice. "Tell me one way you're not perfect."

The only thing she could think of was the fact that she'd been friends with him for fifteen years and was too afraid to ever tell him how she felt about him.

But she wasn't going to do that now either.

Sadie cleared her throat, desperately trying to think of something else to say.

"I didn't stay in touch with you for six years," she finally offered. "I'd say that's pretty imperfect."

A sad smile tugged at the corner of Carter's lips, a smile that quickly fluctuated into a frown. "That street went both ways, didn't it?"

Sadie opened her mouth, wondering if this was the time to talk about what happened.

Before Sadie could say anything, Carter's phone buzzed.

He mumbled, "Excuse me," before pulling it out and glancing at the screen. As he did, his eyes widened.

Sadie glanced over his shoulder, anxious to see what caused his reaction.

A grainy video had been texted to him.

A woman who looked just like Allison stared at the camera and muttered, "It's all your fault."

Then the screen switched to static.

CHAPTER FIFTEEN

CARTER WATCHED the video over and over again. Was that Allison? Could it really be?

"Carter . . ." Sadie's voice faded. "What are you thinking?"

He ran a hand over his face. "I don't know what to think. What does this even mean?"

"Someone is playing with your head," Sadie said.

"This woman said, 'It's all your fault.'" The words lodged in his throat as a burn started there. "It's almost like Allison's ghost is coming back from the grave to haunt me."

"You don't believe in ghosts." Sadie squeezed his forearm and kept her hand there. "Carter, you know her accident wasn't your fault, right?"

The truth was, he didn't know that at all. Every

day since it happened—every single day—Carter thought about it and wished he could go back to do things differently.

"I should have never said those things to her." The words sounded choked as they left his lips.

"Allison was a grown woman. She shouldn't have been driving like she was. She knew better. She was being reckless, and the only person to blame for that is her."

"But I set her off. If I had just been a little wiser with my words—"

"Carter, look at me."

His gaze flickered to Sadie. He saw that determined look in her eyes. Her firm voice indicated she meant business.

"It wasn't your fault. If Allison was still here, she would tell you not to blame yourself."

Carter wanted to laugh, but he couldn't. This wasn't a laughing matter, even if Sadie's words were far-fetched. "I'm not so sure about that."

"I am." Sadie said the words with such assurance that Carter almost believed her for a moment.

"Maybe Allison wants to make me pay for all the heartache I caused her."

"Carter, you tried to make your relationship with Allison work. You sacrificed your own desires in order to make her happy. I know that it can go both ways sometimes. That's what relationships are like—give and take. But Allison would never ever have wished this on you. Anyone who knew you both would tell you that."

"Sadie . . ." Carter hung his head and rubbed his temples as the pressure began to build in him. "I appreciate the fact that you believe in me but—"

"Carter, you've got to stop beating yourself up. Do you think doing this is some kind of penance for what happened? That if you're never happy that that's the justice you deserve over what happened?"

His breath caught. He never thought about it on a conscious level. Sadie's words made sense. Maybe he *was* punishing himself, always keeping happiness at arm's length because he thought he didn't deserve it.

His gaze met Sadie's again. "I don't know what to say."

"You don't have to say anything," she said. "Just know that I'm here for you."

Sadie felt like his rock right now. Then again, she always had been.

He'd felt lost all these years without her.

"Now you need to stop watching this video." Sadie took the phone from his hands. "We need to make sure that Cassidy sees this. What do you say you and I take a trip down to the station to talk to her?"

CASSIDY GLANCED up from the phone to Carter then Sadie as they sat on the other side of her desk at the police station. "You just got this video?"

"That's right," Carter said. "It came to me via text message about fifteen minutes ago."

Cassidy pressed her lips together and slowly shook her head. "How did this person even get your number?"

Carter shrugged. "I'm not sure. But it's not like I keep it secret. That said, my number isn't public either."

"How long have you had this number?"

"Since I moved here."

Cassidy frowned and put the phone down. "I'm liking this less and less all the time."

"You and me both." Carter leaned back and let out a breath. "I still can't believe this is happening. It feels surreal."

"I do have an update while you're here," Cassidy started, lacing her fingers together on her desk.

Sadie sat up straighter. Updates were good. She hoped that Cassidy had something helpful that she might be able to share, something that could lead them to answers.

"My friend who's the medical examiner in Tennessee gave me a call back," Cassidy started. "He examined the autopsy report on Allison. He reviewed all the aspects of the case, and—I'm not sure if I should apologize or if this is a reason to celebrate—but Allison really did die in that accident. Her dental records match. Her DNA. The accident was horrific, but she was still identifiable."

Sadie glanced at Carter in time to see his face fall. He'd been halfway hoping she was still alive, wasn't he?

Sadie generally considered herself someone who knew what to say in difficult situations. It was part of her job. But, right now, she felt speechless. She'd assumed when Carter broke up with Allison that he hadn't loved her anymore. It appeared she was wrong.

She cleared her throat and finally asked, "What are you thinking, Carter?"

He shook his head, the action entirely too somber for her comfort. "I'm with Cassidy. Part of me is relieved to know that she isn't the one stalking us."

Sadie held her breath, waiting for what he would say next. When he didn't say anything else, she finished for him. "And another part of you was hoping that Allison was still alive?"

The quiet words left a bitter taste in her mouth. If Allison was alive, would Carter drop everything and run back to her? Would the bond she and Carter had quickly reignited over the past couple of days mean nothing? Would Carter leave Sadie in the dust again for the beautiful, flashy Allison?

Sadie hated that she even had to ask herself these questions. But they pounded in her head until she couldn't ignore them.

"That's a hard question to answer." Carter rubbed his jaw and looked out the window, his gaze dimming. "If I have a choice between a friend living or dying, of course, I'm going to choose living. Then again, I didn't want Allison to be behind these things that were happening. That would mean she'd turned into a horrible person."

Sadie released her breath. Carter's words made sense. He hadn't totally lost all his logic. But she had to wonder if Carter was in love with Allison still.

"But there's another question that remains."

Cassidy shifted in her seat. "If this woman behind these acts isn't Allison—and I think we all agree that we can rule her out at this point—then who is she?"

"That's a great question," Carter murmured. "I wish I knew."

"Carter and I tried to talk through some suspects earlier." Sadie attempted to keep her thoughts focused on this immediate danger. "Carter was able to list a couple of fans who've messaged him sounding very off-kilter in some ways."

"I'm going to need to look at those names and see if there is any way we can pinpoint anyone who merits further investigation."

"That's a good idea," Carter said. "But other than a crazy fan, I don't know who else this woman could be. I haven't made very many enemies. I think I would have definitely noticed if I had made an enemy who looked like Allison."

"That's the other thing that perplexes me." Cassidy shook her head, her lips still pressed in thought as she paused. "Why would someone try to impersonate Allison in order to hurt you?"

The question hung in the air.

Sadie wished she had the answer. But she had no clue.

CHAPTER SIXTEEN

AS CARTER and Sadie stepped out of the police station, the rain started again. Thankfully, the wind had died, so the sheets of water were no longer coming down sideways. The pitter-patter of the drops had always sounded comforting to Carter, as did the scent of the storm mixed with the ocean. The briny yet fresh scent seemed to open his lungs.

He hoped the storm didn't knock out their cell lines, as often happened here on Lantern Beach. Not only was the ecosystem fragile, but so was the infrastructure at times. The smallest storm could flood roads, cut electricity, and cause other damage.

Carter pushed open an umbrella Cassidy had let them borrow and held it over Sadie. "My lady."

She giggled and scooted closer. "You're so silly."

"Would you like me to lay down my coat for you so that puddle doesn't soak your shoes?"

"You don't have a coat, and, no, that's sweet but ridiculous."

"Don't say I didn't offer."

She giggled again. "I won't."

She looped her arm through his—no doubt out of practicality—and scooted closer so they could share the umbrella.

Carter had to admit that he liked the feeling of Sadie being so close beside him. He liked the scent of peaches that drifted from her hair. Liked the soft feel of her skin when they hugged. Liked the way his stomach flip-flopped every time she smiled.

Mostly, he just liked Sadie.

But he was still mulling over Cassidy's confirmation that Allison had died in that car accident. He didn't quite know what to do about it, and a moment of mourning washed over him again as he remembered his loss.

"I guess we should get back to the apartment," Sadie said above the sound of the raindrops that pounded on the red umbrella.

Going back to the apartment held no appeal to

Carter at the moment. His soul felt like it needed to breathe.

"How do you feel about going for a walk in the rain?" The idea was spontaneous, but it sparked a certain excitement in him. Maybe that was just what he needed to clear his head. Walking always did that for him.

"A walk in the rain?" Sadie looked up at him and raised her eyebrows.

He shrugged, knowing Sadie was the type who liked cathartic moments—unlike Allison who'd loved keeping busy. Allison had never been one who liked to be still or take time to reflect. At first, their differences had felt refreshing. But after time, Carter had realized that Allison's vanity was only going to lead her to disappointment.

Carter snapped back to reality and his invitation to walk in the rain. He looked over at Sadie and shrugged. "You know, for old time's sake."

A grin spread across Sadie's face—a grin that Carter craved. The thought of seeing that every day made his heart do flips.

"Let's do it," Sadie said.

Instead of walking to his apartment, they headed to the boardwalk, remaining close under the umbrella. Carter scanned everything around him. As much as he'd like to pretend like this was a care-free moment, he still needed to be on guard.

There was a lot that could go wrong. There was no telling what this woman who'd been taunting him might do next.

Was she watching them now?

Carter surveyed the area again but didn't see anyone suspicious.

He hoped he wasn't being naive or putting Sadie in danger. He'd never forgive himself if he was.

Allison was a case in point of that. Carter had a hard time letting things go—especially guilt.

But what if Sadie was right? What if it *was* time to let those things go? Even if he wanted to, was forgiving himself something that he could truly do?

For now, he and Sadie continued walking. Carter hummed as they sauntered, a tune repeating in his mind.

I saw her on the sidewalk as I was packing up my bags. And the weight of what I had to do only made my spirit sag. I can remember just how beautiful she had always been. So I wish that I could travel away to the great back when.

"These were some of my favorite times with you." Sadie's voice broke him from his thoughts.

At her words, Carter's mind was swept back to when they were in high school and college. Allison had never been one for getting wet. She said it made her hair frizzy.

But Sadie . . . she was always up for an adventure. If Carter wanted to find a waterfall so he could absorb its scent and deepen the lyrics to a new song, she was there. If he needed to feel sand between his toes, she went along for the ride. Once she'd even gone with him on a road trip to the Grand Canyon.

The two of them had never failed to find adventures and things to chuckle about along the way.

Carter hadn't even realized how much he had missed her.

But he also felt as if a big elephant stood between them. When were they going to talk about the fact that they'd lost touch for so many years? Did Sadie have hard feelings toward him for that? And, if so, would she ever forgive him?

He didn't know the answers to those questions.

He needed to find out.

Later.

SADIE COULD GET LOST in moments like these.

She loved the spontaneity. She loved being able to jump into a moment and embrace it. She loved the scent of the rain and the smell of the sea and the sound of drops hitting the umbrella above them.

Mostly, she loved the warmth emanating from Carter. She held on to his arm as they nestled beneath the umbrella. The moment might have seemed romantic, but the two of them were just friends.

Just as they had always been.

Sadie needed to keep herself in check before she left this place heartbroken. Her goal had been to get over Carter. To move on and find someone else to date.

That hadn't happened. And seeing Carter now reminded her of why.

Because there was no one else out there like Carter Denver. No one she'd ever connected with like him.

But she needed to be smart. Just because she felt warm, fuzzy feelings didn't mean there was anything between them. She talked to her clients about misunderstandings like this all the time. Gave them advice about guarding their hearts while living life to the fullest.

Yet here Sadie was pining after a man who was in

love with one of her best friends—a best friend who was dead.

Could she be any more off her rocker?

If any of her clients had said that aloud, Sadie would have chastised them. Reminded them that they needed to practice self-love—the humble kind like what was mentioned in the Bible. Reminded them not to be so hard on themselves.

But Sadie knew her advice wasn't easy.

Carter paused by a wooden swing facing the ocean and stared out at the raging waves. The scenery in front of them really was beautiful. But as the wind picked up, it brought bursts of cool air from over the water.

"I guess we should get back." Carter almost sounded regretful that they had to leave. "I'd hate for you to catch a cold being out here with me like this."

"I guess we should." She understood his reluctance to leave. Who wouldn't like staring at this all day? A rainy day at the beach was still better than a sunny day in the suburbs. In Sadie's estimation, at least.

They were both silent as they started walking back to Carter's apartment. As they strolled, Sadie's phone buzzed.

She'd gotten a new email about her podcast. She quickly scanned it and sucked in a breath.

"What is it?" Carter paused.

"I accept questions from my listeners," Sadie explained. "I just got a new one from someone. She asked what a person was supposed to do if they loved someone enough to kill for them."

"That's messed up. You think this has something to do with what's going on here?"

Sadie shook her head. "I don't know."

"If that's true, then this person knows who you are too, Sadie. That means you're in even more danger than I originally thought."

She swallowed hard. She'd already had that realization.

Carter looked around. "Let's get you inside."

He took her elbow and their pace quickened. Thankfully, his apartment wasn't far away.

As she stepped inside, Sadie began to release the breath she'd been holding since she'd gotten that email. She braced herself for a greeting from Bo. The dog made her feel more relaxed.

But Bo never came.

Carter seemed to realize his dog was strangely absent at the same time Sadie did, and the two exchanged a glance.

"Bo!" Carter called.

The dog still didn't come.

Something was wrong, Sadie realized.

After everything that had happened, she dreaded finding out what.

CHAPTER SEVENTEEN

"STAY HERE," Carter muttered to Sadie as alarm raced through him.

Something was seriously wrong.

He had to find Bo. Had to figure out what had happened.

The dog *always* came to the door when Carter came in.

A strange scent filled his nostrils.

Was that . . . smoke?

Carter rushed down the hall, worst-case scenarios roaring through his mind. He had to make sure his dog was okay.

He threw open the first bedroom door.

Nothing.

The second door.

Also nothing.

Finally, he threw open his door.

Still nothing.

When Carter reached the bathroom, he saw flames rising from the sink.

Alarm raced through him. Who would have done this?

But he knew. Allison's doppelganger had done this.

She'd been trying to send him a message.

It had worked.

He had to go grab a fire extinguisher. Now. He didn't have any time to waste or his whole place might go up in flames.

But before he could move, Sadie appeared. She held the extinguisher in her hands. Quickly, Carter took it from her and rushed into the bathroom. He sprayed the flames until they died.

He released his breath.

The fire was out.

Smoke still hung in the air, clinging to the ceiling.

But the only damage appeared to be his sink.

This could have been much worse.

But Carter still needed to find his dog . . . and to

figure out how someone had gotten into his apartment.

"THIS LADY ISN'T GIVING up, is she?" Sadie folded her arms across her chest as they waited outside for Cassidy to come.

Another day, another police report. Actually, this would be the second one for the day. Maybe— another hour, another police report was more accurate.

How long was this craziness going to continue? Sadie had no idea. She only knew that it was making her very uneasy.

How far would this person take things? Would the woman not stop until Carter was dead?

And where was sweet Bo?

Sadie pulled her arms more tightly across her chest and glanced at Carter as he paced in front of her. Every once in a while, he called for his dog and whistled.

But Bo never came.

Sadie prayed that this psycho hadn't hurt the dog. The animal was innocent in this. Sadie also knew that the canine was one of the few comforts

Carter had. Her friend's whole demeanor relaxed as soon as he began rubbing his dog's head.

Dogs were good for that. There was a reason they were known as man's best friend.

Just then, Cassidy pulled up in her police SUV. As she stepped out, the expression on her face made it clear she didn't like this any more than they did. It felt good knowing the police chief was on their side and doing everything she could to help.

"I need to clear your apartment, just so we can be certain no one is hiding inside," she started.

Carter motioned for her to go inside. Ten minutes later, she came back out.

"It's clear." Cassidy paused in front of them and frowned. "I'm thinking we need to set up some security cameras outside the apartment. This person isn't backing off."

Carter shrugged, his gaze almost seeming preoccupied or withdrawn. Had everything finally gotten to him? Would this be the offense that finally broke him?

Please, Lord. Be with him. This is a lot for anyone to bear.

"Whatever you think," he finally said.

"I wish I was joking, but I'm not." Cassidy glanced around the street in front of Carter's apartment again. "If this continues, we're definitely going to need to take some more proactive measures. Having one of my officers drive past every ten or fifteen minutes isn't doing the trick. How did someone even get inside your place?"

Sadie cleared her throat. "I looked at the doorknob, just to see if there were any signs someone had picked the lock. I didn't see anything suspicious. Then again, I'm not trained for this."

"I keep a spare key underneath my potted plant." Carter nodded down at a yellow mum that had been planted in a cheerful blue pot near his front door.

Carter had planted a flower? He was always full of surprises.

It was one more thing Sadie loved about him.

Slipping on a glove, Cassidy moved the planter.

The key was gone.

Carter frowned and let out a long, drawn-out breath full of self-reprimand. "I guess I shouldn't have left it there. But I almost forgot I even did. I hardly ever have to use it. And now Bo . . ."

"Maybe the dog ran away when a stranger entered your apartment," Cassidy said. "There's a good chance he's fine. We just need to find him."

Carter shook his head. "I'm sick to my stomach

just thinking about something bad happening to him."

"You know what?" Cassidy's eyes brightened. "I've got it under control here. My guys and I will check things out and look for fingerprints. I can get your statement a little bit later. Why don't you and Sadie go look for Bo?"

Carter seemed to instantly perk at the suggestion. "That sounds good."

"But I also need you to keep your eyes open for trouble," Cassidy reminded them. "I don't like where this is going. And I refuse to have any more casualties on this island."

CHAPTER EIGHTEEN

"BO!" Carter called as they walked down the boardwalk.

They'd been walking beneath the umbrella up and down the boardwalk and the surrounding areas for the past hour. Both he and Sadie were drenched, but there had been no sign of Bo.

Anybody they'd crossed paths with, they'd inquired about the dog. No one had seen him.

It was strange. It wasn't like Bo to run away.

Which just left Carter with the realization that someone had taken him.

His stomach clenched. What had this woman done with his dog?

Carter wasn't going to give up until he found Bo. That was a given.

But he couldn't expect Sadie to go along with him for all of this, especially not in this weather and in these circumstances.

"Listen, why don't I take you back to the apartment so you can rest?" As soon as the words left Carter's lips, he questioned them. Considering everything that had happened, maybe that wasn't the best idea. "On second thought, I could take you to one of my friend's houses to stay until this blows over."

Sadie shook her head, her hair swishing over her shoulders at the action as determination filled her gaze. "I'm not leaving you. We're going to find Bo. He's around here somewhere."

"I wish I felt as confident as you did. But the woman behind this . . . she's unhinged. I don't even know what to think."

"Try to keep your thoughts positive," Sadie said.

"I've been trying, but I'm about to give up."

"Don't do that. We're going to do this. We're going to find Bo."

"What did I ever do without you in my life?" As soon as Carter said the words, regret filled him. The conversation reminded him of what a terrible friend he'd been.

"I'm here now," Sadie said. "That's what's important."

Carter nodded, but the guilt still haunted him.

After they walked down the boardwalk again, they finally ducked beneath the awning of a toy store. Sadie looked up at him. "What do you think we should do now? Do you want to keep searching this area or should we expand?"

Carter sucked on the side of his cheek for a moment in thought. "I want to keep looking, but maybe I need a better plan. We've hit this area already—more than once. Maybe we should go somewhere new."

"I think that's a good idea. But where?"

"We can check out some of the businesses on the other side of the street, near where The Crazy Chefette is. It's worth a shot, right?"

"That's right. Let's do it."

———

TWO HOURS LATER, there was still no sign of Bo. Even Sadie, who considered herself an optimist, felt herself losing hope. But she didn't tell Carter that.

"Maybe we should go check in on things at your place." It wasn't that she wanted to give up. But the rain had long-since soaked through their clothing, the wind grew chillier, and it was getting dark outside.

Carter stared off into the distance before running a hand over his mouth and chin. "I don't want to give up, Sadie."

His words touched her. Someone who cared this much about his dog . . . it showed something about his character. But that came as no surprise to Sadie. She'd already known what a great guy he was.

"If you want to look more, I'll be right here with you."

Carter smiled at Sadie in a way that made her heart warm and made all the sacrifices worth it. Wasn't that what relationships—friendships—were about? Looking out for one another?

Carter had always looked out for Allison. He'd been a shining example of love. It was too bad that Allison never returned the gesture.

"Thank you, Sadie," he murmured. "For everything."

Her cheeks heated—a dead giveaway if Carter noticed. She quickly looked away and nodded, knowing she needed to change the subject. "Of course. Where do you want to look now?"

"The only other place I can think of is on the

beach itself. I know as soon as we go on the other side of that sand dune, it's going to get even colder. Are you sure you're up for it?"

"Of course." The thought of it made her muscles tense. There was nothing worse than being wet in the wind.

But Sadie would make that sacrifice for Carter.

Sure enough, as soon as they crossed the dune, the wind inverted their umbrella. From here on out, they were going to have to walk in the torrential downpour.

Carter took her hand, not as much as a romantic gesture as it was just to keep them together in this storm.

As the weather got worse and the sun went down, their chances of finding Bo seemed to grow slimmer and slimmer. But Sadie wouldn't give up until Carter did.

"What's that over there?" Sadie pointed to a structure in the distance.

"That's the stage we have set up for some of the concerts here. It's the base of it, at least. The bigger the concert, the more platforms they add onto it."

"Maybe we should go look over there. Is it all open to the elements?"

"There is a storage room in the back where they keep some equipment. It couldn't hurt to check."

They both leaned forward as they walked into the wind and rain. Even Sadie's bones felt cold right now.

But she wasn't going to complain.

Finally, they reached the stage area.

"Bo!" Sadie called.

She was so used to hearing nothing when she called the dog's name that she wasn't surprised when she heard nothing but the wind this time.

Carter pulled her around to the back side of the building where the storage area was located. A little ramp had been set up there, and they climbed toward the door that swung out.

Why was that door open anyway? It seemed if there was equipment in there, it would be locked.

As they reached the top of the ramp, a new sound filled Sadie's ears.

Was that a bark?

It was hard to hear over the downpour around them.

But Sadie was nearly certain that's what she'd heard.

Carter released her hand and stepped inside the

storage area. His face lit as he looked at something in the back.

"Bo!"

Sadie stepped inside behind him and saw that the dog had been tied up in the corner of the room, in between some music stands and wooden boxes.

She let out a sigh of relief. From her vantage point, the canine appeared to be fine.

"Thank goodness." As soon as Sadie muttered the words, a creak sounded behind her.

The door swung shut, slamming with force.

Had the wind caught it?

That's what Sadie wanted to believe.

But as she reached for it and pushed, the wood didn't budge.

It was as she feared.

Someone must have been waiting for them.

And now she and Carter were locked inside.

CHAPTER NINETEEN

"WHAT?" Carter rushed toward the door and shoved it.

It didn't budge. In the darkness, it was nearly impossible to see the handle, to see if there was any other way out.

He knew the truth—someone had locked them in here.

And he knew exactly who it was.

Allison's doppelganger.

She must have been waiting for him and Sadie to come. This had been part of her plan this whole time.

What sense did it make?

He pounded on the door and yelled, "Hey! Let us out!"

"Carter?" He heard Sadie's voice. For one of the first times since he'd known Sadie, she sounded almost fragile.

He reached through the opaque air until he felt her arm. "I'm here."

She scooted closer, nestling up beside him as the rain thundered overhead. Since they were already wet, the cool air made them feel even chillier. And the darkness brought with it the impeding feeling of the unknown.

"I don't like where this is going, Carter," Sadie muttered.

"Me either. We've got to figure out a way to get out of here before this woman does something else erratic."

"That door's pretty solid."

"We can call somebody," Carter said. "Cassidy. She can be here in five minutes."

The relief from Sadie was almost palpable. "Yes. Of course. That makes sense."

Carter reached into his pocket and pulled out his phone. But when he dialed, nothing happened.

"No . . ." He tried again to the same result.

"What's going on?" Sadie's voice cracked as she asked the question.

"The cell tower must have been taken out."

"Could the timing be any worse?"

Sadie's face, full of worry, appeared in the fading light from his cell phone. "I'm sorry, Sadie."

"It's okay." But her voice almost sounded resigned—something he rarely heard from her. "Let's work on getting Bo loose. Then we'll figure out how to get out of here."

Carter handed her his phone. "Can you shine the light on the corner for me while I see if I can find something to undo this rope?"

"Of course." Sadie stood beside Bo, rubbing his head. The dog lapped up the attention and leaned into her.

Bo seemed to like Sadie almost as much as Carter liked Sadie. Ordinarily that thought would make him smile. Right now, there was too much on the line.

He looked through some of the boxes stored here. Anything metal couldn't be kept in this space. The area wasn't climate controlled and entirely too humid. Most of the boxes were built to set amplifiers and things of that sort on. Occasionally, someone accidentally left some of their equipment back here, though. That's what Carter needed to find right now.

Finally, he found a hammer inside one of the

wooden boxes. It wasn't much, but the tool would work.

Holding it in his hand, Carter went to the corner where Bo had been secured to one of the tie downs. Using the tool, he whacked at the wooden knob for several moments until it came loose. Finally, the knob fell to the ground and Bo was free.

His dog jumped on Carter and began licking his face almost as if he knew what had just happened.

"It's good to see you too, boy," Carter muttered. "Now we've got to figure out a way to get us out of here."

Sadie glanced at his phone again, the light again illuminating her face. "We still can't make calls. Do you think we can beat our way out of here with that hammer?"

Carter seriously doubted it. But they didn't have very many options right now. "It's worth a shot, but I don't have much hope that it will help. If nothing else, we can use it as a weapon."

He hoped it didn't come down to that. But he had no idea what to expect.

The fact that Allison's doppelganger had been quiet ever since she'd locked them in here spoke volumes.

What was she planning?

Carter only knew they had to get out of here before she enacted it.

———————

"I DON'T LIKE THIS, CARTER." Sadie's voice had a slight tremble to it as she stood near the door.

She told herself it was because of the cold, but it was also partly the situation. To say she felt unnerved would be an understatement.

"Neither do I." Carter leaned closer as they stood in front of each other. Sadie crept toward him, desperate for something—or someone—to ground her right now.

All she could see was darkness.

"We're going to figure out something to do here," Carter said. "We will."

It was almost like the roles had been reversed. Carter was the one trying to talk some sense into Sadie. She wasn't complaining.

They had tried the door again. It hadn't budged.

They'd tried to use the hammer to beat through a wall. That hadn't worked either.

They'd yelled some more and tried to be as loud as possible. But Sadie knew nobody could hear them over the wind outside.

Every few minutes, they checked their phones. But the lines were still down. Sadie knew that, most likely, cell towers wouldn't be back up until the storm passed—probably even a little later than that.

She was out of ideas, and her worry was beginning to grow, despite her resistance.

"Hey." Carter's voice sounded prodding and full of concern. "I know you're cold. Come sit down."

She wanted to argue, but he took her hand and tugged her closer. The two of them sat side by side and leaned against the wall behind them. As they did, Bo put his chin on Carter's leg and waited, seeming just as perturbed as they were.

Carter slipped his arm around Sadie's shoulder and pulled her closer. She welcomed the extra heat coming from his body as they sat silently beside each other for several minutes.

There was so much Sadie wanted to say. Was this the time? Was this their opportunity to talk about everything that had happened between them?

What if they didn't get out of this alive? If that was the case, then what did she have to lose by speaking what was on her heart?

Nothing, she realized.

Sadie opened her mouth to speak, but, before she could, a sound caught her ear.

Carter swung the light from his phone toward the door.

Something had been slipped underneath it.

"Do you see that?" She pointed at the object. "I don't remember that being there before."

Carter leaned forward to grab it. As he did, Sadie instantly missed his warmth.

She'd missed her opportunity to talk to him also, she realized.

But there was no going back now. She only prayed they had time later, that it wasn't too late.

Carter pulled the object toward them before slipping an arm around Sadie again.

She turned on the light on her phone and saw it was a zip lock bag full of what appeared to be papers. Carter opened the seal and slid the contents out onto the floor between them.

Sadie shook her head at what she saw there.

Photos. Photos of Carter, Allison, and Sadie.

Except each of the pictures had been torn in half, separating the images of the threesome. And the person that had been torn from the other two was . . . Sadie.

"Why would someone do this?" Carter's voice sounded wispy with shock . . . and anger.

Sadie released her breath as realization hit her.

"To make you suffer more. That's what this has all been about."

"To make me suffer?"

"Carter, I don't know why I didn't see this sooner," Sadie rushed, her thoughts rapidly clicking into place. "This person is reenacting your songs."

"What do you mean?"

She held up the pictures. "This represents your song 'Photos of What Had Once Been.'"

"Keep going."

"You said you saw Allison on the sidewalk at your concert? She was acting out 'Sidewalk Dreams.' When she almost ran us over? 'Blindsided by Love.' What happened today at your place? 'Fire in the House.'"

"Wow. I think you're right." Carter shook his head, his eyes wide and almost dumbfounded. "But I still don't understand how this makes me suffer."

"This person has hit you over the head. Tried to make you feel guilty over Allison. Tried to take away your dog. And now they're trying to make you feel bad because of our fractured friendship. Because I was the third wheel."

"I never thought of you as that," he said.

Sadie shrugged, knowing he told the truth. Carter had never made her feel like an outsider.

But Allison had.

"I didn't say that you ever treated me like that," Sadie said. "But this person obviously thinks so."

Sadie made a mental note. The person behind this obviously knew a lot of their history. That only meant one thing.

This person must go pretty far back in her and Carter's lives.

In fact, maybe this wasn't someone that only Carter knew.

Would Sadie have known this woman also?

CHAPTER TWENTY

CARTER LICKED HIS LIPS, trying to find the right words. The image of those pictures—of Sadie being torn out of them—caused acid to rise in his stomach.

If the person who'd left these had been trying to strike a nerve, she had succeeded.

He cleared his throat as he tried to figure out how to make this right. He couldn't put off these conversations any longer. "I'm sorry I lost touch with you, Sadie."

She shrugged it off, but her voice sounded mellow as she said, "It's okay."

"But it wasn't okay. You were my best friend, and I basically pulled away and stopped talking to you." Carter turned his phone's flashlight back on and set it beside them.

Her gaze met his, and Carter saw something slightly broken there. It wasn't an emotion he saw on Sadie very often. The only other times he remembered it was when her parents had gotten divorced, then again at Allison's funeral.

That was the last time they'd seen each other. They'd grieved together.

They'd gone their separate ways not to really speak again.

"Why didn't you call?" Sadie's voice sounded fragile as her question filled the space between them.

Carter let out a breath and rested his head against the wall. "Maybe I was too busy beating myself up. Maybe I figured you wouldn't want to be my friend anymore. We were drifting apart before Allison died."

"Why did we let that happen?"

"I ask myself that all the time. It's just kind of the way everything worked out. Allison and I going off on our own. You staying at college. We were going in different directions."

"That didn't mean you couldn't stay in touch. I did try to call."

"And I tried to call you back after that . . . at first. But then I had late nights on the road. Meanwhile, you had a normal schedule. We just couldn't seem to find the time to meet up. Or maybe that was just an excuse. I don't really know." Carter swung his head with regret. He'd justified his actions at the time, told himself they were growing apart.

But he'd actually made his biggest mistake ever.

"What would it be an excuse for?" Sadie's voice was almost a whisper as she asked the question.

Carter cleared his throat again. "The truth was, I came to the point in my life where I felt like I had to choose between you and Allison."

He thought he'd feel better revealing the truth. Instead, Carter felt like he'd been punched in the gut. He had no one to blame for the feeling except himself. He had to live with the consequences of his decisions.

"What does that mean?" Sadie asked. "I would have never made you choose between me and Allison."

Carter nodded slowly, an unseen weight pressing on him. "Exactly. And Allison . . ."

"She gave you an ultimatum?"

"In so many words, yes. She said if we wanted to make our music work, we had to give everything to it, to stop looking back."

"Why would she say that?"

Carter licked his lips. "Because she suspected that . . . I liked you."

Sadie didn't say anything for a moment, as if uncertain she'd heard him correctly. "No, you liked Allison."

"I liked you first, Sadie. I was just always too afraid to tell you. Then Allison appeared. She came on strong, and I was just kind of swept away in the romance of it. Being with her but seeing you? That was hard."

Carter paused and waited, anxious to see how Sadie was going to respond.

Because he'd vowed to never say those things out loud. To never risk ruining his friendship with Sadie by throwing out how he had really felt.

But his words were true.

From the moment Sadie sat at that lunch table with him in high school, she'd inspired him to do bigger and better things. She'd inspired him to believe in himself. To be his best.

And in return, Carter had been totally infatuated.

Just like those other boys he'd talked about who'd followed Sadie around like lost puppy dogs.

Carter had been one of them.

And Sadie had been clueless about it.

And, in some ways, those feelings had never gone away.

Not even now.

Especially not now.

———

SADIE'S HEART pounded in her ears. Had she just heard Carter correctly? Certainly, she hadn't.

Because it almost sounded like Carter had just said that he had liked her.

In past tense.

Right?

Sadie licked her lips. "I had no idea."

"I know," Carter murmured. "You were one of the most important people in my life. I didn't want to ruin that."

"I wish you would have told me."

"I wish I'd told you too," Carter murmured.

Sadie turned toward him. She knew she had to look horrible. She felt wet tendrils of her hair clinging to her face, neck, and shoulders. She felt her shirt hugging her arms and chest. The rain had seemed to reactivate the scent of her shampoo, and now the fresh scent of peaches rose around them.

That wasn't even to mention how Carter looked.

He looked great.

Of course.

They could be soaking wet, and he'd still look great. Even though rain still glistened in his hair and on his beard, his eyes were what drew Sadie in.

They always had.

There was so much depth there, so much emotion. None of the other guys she'd met ever had that. They'd been too caught up in being manly—not that Carter wasn't manly. But he had a sensitive side that drew Sadie to him.

Sadie swallowed hard, her throat aching at the motion. "I could have tried harder to stay in touch also. The truth is, maybe there was part of me that was . . . jealous."

"Jealous of what?" Surprise laced his voice.

"You and Allison. There were times I felt like she'd taken you away from me. And, as much as I always tried to be the bigger person, it was hard. Sometimes, I resented your relationship."

Carter squeezed Sadie's hand. "It's okay to let people know that you have weaknesses. In fact, it makes me feel a whole lot better about myself to know that you aren't perfect."

"I was telling the truth earlier when I told you I was far from perfect. Maybe I just hide my flaws better than other people. But the truth was, it was easier to stay in school and to not go on tour with you guys because it was too hard to see you two together."

Carter's eyes widened. "You mean that?"

Sadie let out a self-conscious chuckle. "Yes. Because I liked you from the first day we met too. Then Allison swept into our lives, and, well . . . we both know how Allison was. We both loved her. But she also liked everything to be about her. What she wanted, she got."

Carter let out a burst of air, his voice somber as he said, "Yes, she did. Nobody could deny that. Not even Allison."

"When you didn't return my calls and we lost touch, I figured it was for the best." Sadie's voice sounded thin, even to her own ears. Emotions hovered just beneath the surface—emotions that had been trying to emerge for years. "I figured I should try to move on."

"Did you?" Carter's voice caught.

Sadie glanced up at him, feeling something quake inside her. She was on the edge of saying something that could change her life. For the best or for the worst—if she and Carter got out of here alive, that was.

"No other guy ever measured up to you." There. Sadie had said it. She'd told Carter what had been on her mind all these years.

Her hand went to her stomach as soon as the words left her mouth, and she feared she might throw up.

Maybe she shouldn't have shared how she really felt. What if things were never the same between them now? What if Carter didn't feel the same way?

"Sadie . . ." Carter murmured, his voice husky.

He released her hand and, instead, cupped her face. Their gazes met, and an ocean of memories and emotions passed between them. Their bond was so strong that it nearly felt visible.

Time seemed suspended between them as Carter leaned closer. Sadie's heart pounded in her chest as she anticipated feeling his lips against hers.

She'd dreamed about this moment for a long time.

Maybe too long.

Slowly, Carter's lips brushed hers. When she didn't pull away, he pressed harder until his mouth consumed hers.

His hand slipped from her face to around her waist. He tugged her closer. Sadie's arms encircled his neck as all the tension between them dissolved.

Warmth unlike anything Sadie had ever felt filled every part of her. Her veins. Her chest. Her heart felt like it might explode with heat.

But just as the kiss grew deeper, Sadie heard something outside.

It wasn't the wind or the rain or even thunder.

A footstep sounded right outside the door.

She pulled away from Carter and clutched his arm, trying to prepare herself for whatever was about to happen.

CHAPTER TWENTY-ONE

CARTER JUMPED to his feet and pushed Sadie behind him, the moment broken. Beside him, Bo growled. Carter put a hand on Bo's collar to keep his dog from lunging.

The next instant, the door flew open.

Allison stood there, lightning flashing behind her and making her look even crazier than she already was.

Except it wasn't Allison.

It was someone who looked exactly like her.

Almost.

A chill went up Carter's spine at the thought.

He raised his hand and started to charge toward her.

Until he saw the gun the woman was holding.

"Don't even think about it." She scowled at them. "Tie the dog back up. Now!"

"Why are you doing this?" Sadie asked. "Just let us go."

"I can't do that. There are still lessons to learn."

"Maybe we can talk over coffee then." Sadie's voice sounded calm and confident. She had a way of convincing people to do things.

But Carter didn't think it was going to work this time. There wouldn't be any reasoning with this woman.

"Tie the dog up before I shoot him." The woman's voice grew harder with each syllable.

"Okay, okay." Carter raised his free hand. "Just don't hurt anybody."

"Then move." The woman's mouth barely opened as she talked. Instead, her teeth remained clenched as she shot laser beams with her eyes at both of them.

Carter worked quickly, muttering quiet apologies to Bo for tying him back up again. But he couldn't take any chances. The woman was obviously unstable, and she had a gun and they didn't. Though Carter would like to think that Bo could take her out, he wasn't confident that the woman wouldn't pull the trigger first.

He gave the knot another tug before raising his hands and turning back to the woman.

He tried to place where he had seen her before, but he couldn't.

Not yet.

Whatever memory it was, the recollection was close.

"What do you want?" Carter asked. There was no need to play this game any longer than they had to. The woman had obviously come here with some type of game plan.

"I want you to go onstage," she growled.

"Onstage?" What in the world was this woman talking about?

"But first, tie her up." She tossed some rope at him.

"Why would I want to tie Sadie up?" A bad feeling brewed in his gut.

"Because I said so!" The woman's eyes widened until Carter could see the whites all around her pupils. Carter knew that the woman was not in the mood to compromise.

He slowly picked up the rope. As he did, he and Sadie exchanged a glance, and Carter knew that Sadie understood what was about to happen.

He was going to tie her up, just like this woman

had said. He didn't know what was going to play out afterward. But he would fight with everything in him to save Sadie.

For that matter, he had fought with everything in him for Allison too. He just hadn't let himself accept that fact for all these years. It wasn't until Sadie came back into his life that he was able to see things more clearly.

Allison's death wasn't his fault. Allison should have never gone driving down that road at such a high speed that night. Even though he would do everything in his power to turn back time and have Allison back, he had to stop letting that grave hold him down.

But was it too late to make things right?

Sadie gave him a slight nod and then turned around, pressing her wrists together behind her. Carter tried to gently wrap the ropes around her wrists so it wouldn't be too uncomfortable for her. But Allison's doppelganger seemed to notice.

"Tighter!" she snapped. "Don't make me do it myself. Because if you do, I'm going to have to knock you out first."

Sucking in a breath, Carter tightened the ropes.

"I'm sorry," he murmured into Sadie's ear.

"Now the two of you need to follow me," the

woman barked. "Any quick moves, and I won't be afraid to use my gun. Understand?"

"Understood," Carter said.

"You two in front. I'm walking behind you. You need to go onstage. Don't walk too fast."

Carter trudged through the wet sand, trying to keep his pace even so he wouldn't tick off the woman with the gun. Pelting rain hit them, soaking their skin. The wind picked up again and chilled Carter to his bones.

He glanced at Sadie, wishing he could protect her from this.

Maybe he still could. He just had to wait for the right opening—kind of like planning when the bridge of a song would start, only with much more serious consequences if he got it wrong.

As directed, they climbed the steps onto a platform Carter had played on many times before. Would this be his final performance?

A lone chair sat center stage, a guitar leaning against it.

Carter's guitar.

That's what that woman had been doing inside his apartment earlier, in addition to setting the fire. If he'd checked, he would have noticed his guitar was gone—because this woman had taken it and put it on the stage.

"You." The woman stared at Carter. "Sit."

She pointed at the chair using her forehead.

The last thing he wanted to do was to leave Sadie. But it appeared he had no choice. He glanced at her once more and saw the gun pressed to her side. The look on Sadie's face was that of pure terror. He nodded, slowly walked to the chair, and sat down.

"One wrong move and she's dead," the woman growled. "Understand?"

Carter nodded, afraid to set her off—afraid for Sadie's life. "I understand."

He prayed that somehow this evening would take a turn for the better.

Mostly, he prayed that he and Sadie would get out of this alive. If he had to choose only one of them, then Sadie.

He had to keep her safe.

SADIE FELT helpless as she sat on the floor at the edge of the stage with her hands tied. She'd tried to leave space between her wrists as Carter had tied them together. She needed to get these ropes off, but it was going to take some time.

She had no idea what was going to play out over the next few minutes. Part of her didn't want to find out.

Her only prayer was that Cassidy would come looking for them. There was no other way Sadie could foresee she and Carter getting out of this situation alive.

Sadie's gaze latched onto the woman as she paced the stage.

Why did she look familiar? Sadie felt certain she'd seen her somewhere before. But where?

Earlier, Sadie had assumed that the person behind these crimes was someone from their past, someone who knew both Sadie and Carter.

Could Sadie and Carter have known this woman from back in high school or college?

As she studied the woman's face, a realization hit her. If Sadie imagined the woman with dark hair, twenty pounds heavier, and with a longer nose . . . she would almost look like Emily Maddox from high school.

Emily, the girl who'd been madly in love with Carter. Who'd written his name with hearts all around it on her notebooks in calculus class.

It had to be her. Sadie was nearly certain of it.

But now that she knew that information, how could she use it to put an end to this situation?

Sadie was going to have to rely on every bit of her training if she wanted to get out of this alive—if she wanted to get *Carter* out of this alive.

She continued to work at those binds around her wrists. They were becoming looser, but she couldn't slip them off yet.

"Pick up your guitar," Emily growled at Carter.

Carter raised his hands, as if silently begging the woman to slow her impulses. Then he obediently picked up his guitar and rested it on his knee. "What do you want me to do now?"

"I want you to sing 'Hometown Heartaches,'" she said.

"'Hometown Heartaches?'" Surprise laced Carter's voice. "I haven't played that song in years."

"Play it. Now!"

Carter slowly nodded and began to strum the guitar. As he did, Emily held the gun toward him. Occasionally, she glanced back at Sadie, as if daring her to make any kind of move.

Carter's voice didn't sound as strong and soothing as it normally did as he began. His nerves were showing—and that hardly ever happened. He was never as relaxed as he was onstage.

But this situation was different.

"She was a hometown girl. I hardly knew her name. I only knew she was obsessed with my fame. I tried to let her down the easy way, but she's still following me to this day. Oh, she was a hometown girl, but I was no longer a part of that world. How could I tell her that she wasn't my type? And if I did, would it even be right?"

The haunting lyrics echoed across the stage.

Emily thought Carter wrote that song about her, didn't she?

Sadie's mind raced.

This woman was going off the deep end. If Sadie was right, Emily had been obsessing about Carter for the past fifteen years.

That was a lot of time for someone to scheme. A lot of time for anger to build up. A lot of time to develop a plan.

Sadie had no idea what was going to happen.

But it wasn't going to be good.

CHAPTER TWENTY-TWO

AS CARTER STARTED the second verse, a realization tried to form in his head.

He knew who this woman was. The answer was on the cusp of his consciousness. But Carter just couldn't place her at the moment.

Instead, he kept singing, trying to buy time. He had no idea what this woman's plan was. But she was obviously unhinged.

Just as he reached the second verse, he saw the woman's eyes narrow.

The next instant, a bullet rang through the air.

His guitar splintered. Carter gasped and rushed to his feet as the neck of his guitar fractured into what seemed like hundreds of pieces. His strings split and wound through the air, almost as if they were in pain.

But Carter was okay. He hadn't been shot.

His gaze rushed to Sadie.

He released his breath.

Sadie was fine too. But based on the wild look in her eyes, she was as terrified as Carter felt.

"Do you know who I am yet?" The woman stepped closer, the menacing look in her eyes remaining.

Just then, something clicked in his head.

"I didn't write that song about you, Emily," he said.

A strange emotion rolled over her face, almost as if she'd been surprised that Carter remembered her.

"You knew I liked you." The words practically spit from her mouth. "Why couldn't you have liked me too?"

"Sometimes the heart doesn't work like that."

Her scowl deepened. "You couldn't even give me a chance."

"Emily." Carter stepped closer, trying to plead with her, to talk her down from the edge. "You were always a nice girl."

"But you only had eyes for Allison." She rolled her eyes. "I was never good enough for you. Everything was always about her. *Allison, Allison, Allison.* Seeing you with her made me sick to my stomach."

"All of that is over now," Carter reminded her. "Allison is dead."

Instead of looking comforted by the thought, the words only seemed to make Emily angrier. Her face reddened as she stared at Carter. "You still love her, don't you? You're still in love with her. I can hear it in your songs."

"The songs I've written recently aren't about Allison."

"Then who are they about?" Emily demanded.

Carter wanted to say Sadie. But if he did that, he'd be making Sadie a target. He couldn't let that happen. "They're about my dream girl."

Emily's expression seemed to soften. "I want to be your dream girl."

"Then why don't you put down that gun? Let's go talk. Catch up. Just the two of us. There are better ways to do this."

As Emily stared at him, Carter thought he'd gotten through to her. Maybe they could end this peacefully.

He waited to see what she was about to say and prayed he could change Emily's mind.

SADIE COULD TELL Emily was coming even more unhinged. Had Carter's words gotten through to her? Knowing what Sadie did about psychology, she didn't think so.

But she prayed that was the case.

"You've already had your chance!" Emily raised her gun again. "It's too late."

Sadie's heart pounded harder into her chest.

If they didn't do something quickly, Emily was going to shoot Carter. Sadie felt it in her gut. She had to do something.

"You don't want to do this, Emily," Sadie said as she stepped closer.

Emily turned toward Sadie, swinging the gun toward her with nostrils flaring. "Stay out of this. You weren't even supposed to be here."

"But I am here," Sadie said. "And I can help. That's what I do."

Emily rolled her eyes. "Oh, I listen to you and your stupid podcast. Always telling people how they can make their lives better. You make it sound so easy."

"Oftentimes, it's just a matter of changing your mindset," Sadie said. "You know that gun's not going to make anything better right now. It's not going to make Carter love you. It's not going to change anything that happens. The only thing that gun is going to change is your future and the future of whoever is on the receiving end of your bullet."

"Shut up!" The gun trembled in Emily's hands as she still pointed it toward Sadie. "I don't want you to be a part of this. Maybe I should just finish you off now so I can continue my conversation with Carter."

Despite the fact that Emily was coming unraveled, Sadie took another step closer. "I always liked you in high school, Emily. You were smart and funny. A little boy crazy. But I knew that you were having a hard time at home after your parents divorced."

"Shut up. You don't know what you're talking about."

"But I do. My parents divorced too. It's part of the reason I became a life coach. I knew what it was like to struggle, and I wanted to help other people who felt the same way I did."

Emily's gaze seemed to soften for a moment. "There's nothing you can do that will make things better. All I've wanted for all this time is to feel whole. But I need Carter to do it."

"When your dad left, I know it was hard for you," Sadie continued. "But you know a person can't make you feel whole. You can only feel whole with your-self . . . and God."

"*Don't* bring God into this. I've had fifteen years to think about this. And the only thing that brought me any comfort was thinking about Carter and the fact that he and I should be together one day."

Another shot of fear went through Sadie. Thinking about someone for fifteen years and plan-ning a moment like this made it seem unlikely they'd all walk away with any type of solution. Emily needed some serious help.

"If you've been obsessing about Carter for so long, then why are you doing this now? Why are you trying to hurt him?" Sadie continued to try to reach her.

Emily's nostrils flared. "Whatever I've done, he hasn't responded. I knew I had to take extreme measures if I wanted to get his attention."

"You have my attention." Carter leaned toward her, his gaze pleading with her. "But we need to talk this through with words, not violence."

"I want you to write me a song," Emily said.

"What kind of song?" Carter asked.

"A song that shows how you feel about me."

"I don't have a guitar anymore. You shot it."

"You don't need a guitar. Make a song up. Now.

Just you and your voice." Her gun swung back toward him as determination hardened her voice.

Sadie saw Carter swallow hard. Saw the sweat across his forehead.

He obviously realized how serious the situation was. He felt the pressure. Knew the consequences.

Sadie knew that they had to do something soon if either of them wanted to get out of this alive. She'd trained for a lot of things, but she'd never trained for a situation like this.

CHAPTER TWENTY-THREE

CARTER CLEARED HIS THROAT, knowing he didn't work great under pressure. But he had no choice right now but to try to comply.

Emily stared at him, her gun still pointed his way. He had no doubt she'd use it if she saw fit.

He cleared his throat again, trying to think of something to say. He had nothing. He was going to have to wing it.

"Looking for love has never been easy," he started singing, his tone uneven. "Searching for someone is enough to make you queasy. But we've gotta have hope in what a new day will bring. It's the only reason that I can sing—"

"Stop!" Emily yelled. "That's not what I wanted. I want you to write a love song. For *me*. Do it!"

Carter nodded slowly, his mind racing. How could he get out of this? How could he protect Sadie?

The only thing he knew to do was to keep singing—to use his music, the one thing he was best at. To hope somebody else showed up.

Because there was no way he could win—just him against Emily and her gun.

He licked his lips before trying again. "There was a girl who had eyes that looked like sea glass. I longed to talk to her so I asked for a hall pass. I saw my name and hers with hearts all around, and it made me smile, no longer frown . . . Love happens when you're least expecting it. Love happens sometimes right in front of you. Love happens when—"

Carter tried to think of something that rhymed, but his mind went blank.

"Finish it!" Emily yelled.

He wiped his hands on his jeans and tried to think of something. "Love happens when you're least expecting it. Love happens sometimes right in front of you. Love happens, and it makes you stop and see. Love, it happens. It happens, and it brings hope anew."

Sadie, he realized. Not that the lyrics were his best—not by any means.

But he'd been thinking about Sadie when he sang those words.

Because he did love her, and he had for a long time. Now they needed to get through this so he could tell her that.

He wouldn't let her slip away again.

"I want more." The gun trembled in Emily's hand. "I want you to sing with me forever."

Something changed in her eyes.

She had a new plan, Carter realized.

When Emily turned her gun on Sadie, Carter knew exactly what it was.

His worst fears were about to materialize.

SADIE FELT the tremble rush through her.

Emily was going to kill her, get her out of the way. Then Emily was going to force Carter to go with her somewhere.

In this woman's mind, the twisted logic made perfect sense.

But that was only because the woman was unhinged.

Sadie had to try to talk some sense into her.

"You don't want to do this." Sadie's voice wavered.

"I have no choice," Emily's teeth clenched as she said the words.

"You always have a choice. Always."

"Well, there you go again. Ms. Perfect Sadie Thompson. The person everyone loved. Who helped anybody who needed it." She shook her head, almost as if she pitied Sadie. "All these years I thought you were being a fake. But you weren't, were you? You're just a good person."

"I tried to be my best. But I'm far from perfect."

Emily continued to stare at Sadie, as if she didn't believe her.

Sadie had to convince Emily that she was nothing special. "Truthfully, I was always jealous of Allison too. I never liked the way my friend treated Carter. But he seemed so happy. I didn't want to burst his bubble."

"You should have! Then maybe we wouldn't be in the situation we are right now."

Sadie couldn't think about that right now. "You have to let people make their own decisions. If you force them to do what you want them to do, then it's not real. It's not authentic."

"I tried that method and it didn't work!" Emily's

voice continued to rise. "So now I'm doing things my way. And, in order to do things my way, I need to make sure you're out of the picture."

Another stab of fear sliced through her. Sadie's plan wasn't working, and she didn't know what else she could do to stop this. "Emily . . . things aren't going to turn out the way you think they are."

"I guess I'm going to have to see for myself. I've always been an experiencer, as my mom said." Emily raised her gun and aimed it at Sadie's chest.

Sadie braced herself, trying to prepare for the bullet that she fully expected to slice through her body at any minute.

CHAPTER TWENTY-FOUR

CARTER SAW what was about to happen. He had to stop it.

He lunged toward Emily.

Their bodies collided just as the gun fired.

No!

Where had the bullet gone?

Carter glanced at Sadie.

As he did, Emily rammed the gun into his head.

His vision blurred.

"I knew it," she snarled. "You love *her* now."

Carter tried to sit up, tried to find his bearings. But his head spun. He could *not* let the situation get the best of him.

He raised his hand, trying to block Emily from

striking again. One more blow might knock him out and then he'd be no good.

As Carter's vision cleared, he saw that Emily's gun was now aimed at him.

Carter braced himself, knowing that this very well could be the end.

"I did everything for you." Emily's nostrils flared. "I even changed the way I looked so I'd be like Allison."

"Why would you do that?" Carter asked. "You looked fine the way you were."

"Because you obviously are attracted to women who look like Allison. I wanted to be one of those people. I tried to send you letters to get your attention, but they didn't work. I knew I had to take a drastic action."

"So you came here to Lantern Beach? Just to do all of this?" Carter couldn't even begin to fathom the places this woman's mind had gone.

"I thought if I acted out your songs, I would get your attention. Then she showed up." Emily scowled at Sadie.

Carter stole a glance at her and saw Sadie lying on the stage with blood flowing from her arm.

That bullet *had* hit her.

His heart pounded harder. Though Sadie

appeared to be okay, there was nothing okay about being shot. What if she was losing too much blood? He had no time to waste right now.

"If you love me so much, why did you hit me on the head with a crowbar, Emily?" Carter asked.

"You weren't supposed to see me yet. I hadn't put everything in place yet."

Her words sent a chill up his spine. "What do you mean?"

"I mean, I bought a little cottage on the other side of town. It's perfect. Crushed oyster shells lead up the driveway. Wind chimes sing outside. The seagrass blows with the breeze in the flowerbed. If you listen closely, you can even hear the ocean waves."

"Just like 'Paradise in a Bottle,'" Carter mumbled.

It was another one of his songs. This woman hadn't been lying when she'd said she was his biggest fan. She appeared to have memorized all his lyrics.

"Sing my song for me again, Carter."

He glanced at Sadie again. She still lay there, but her eyes were open and wide as she watched everything playing out.

"Emily . . ." Carter started.

"I said, *sing it*." She still pointed the gun at him.

Carter's mind went blank. He could hardly even remember the song he'd just written under duress. But he had to.

He cleared his throat before singing, "Love happens when you're least expecting it. Love happens sometimes right in front of you. Love happens and that makes you stop and see. Love, it happens. It happens and it brings hope anew."

A slow smile spread across Emily's face, and her eyes lit with satisfaction. "It's perfect. I want you to sing it for me all the time. For the rest of our lives."

He swallowed hard. "As we live in a little cottage you bought for us?"

She smiled, the look in her eyes making it clear something was off with her. "That's right. It's going to be perfect."

Carter glanced at Sadie one more time before looking back at Emily. He knew what he had to do. "Let's go there. Just you and me. Together."

He had to figure out a way to get her away from Sadie. This seemed like his best bet.

Emily nodded, a little too anxiously. "Really? Okay. Let's go. You're not trying to pull one over on me, are you? Because I can make you so happy, Carter. Happier than Allison ever did. Happier than

Sadie ever would. You're all I ever think about. I'll live my entire life to make you happy."

A sick feeling bubbled in his gut.

Carter didn't know what he would do once he got to that cottage. All he cared about right now was getting this woman away from Sadie.

That was all that mattered.

SADIE GROANED as pain cut through her arm again. She felt certain the bullet had just skimmed her bicep, but the pain was still incredible.

Now that Emily had turned her back, Sadie pulled her arms from the rope around her wrists. She'd finally managed to loosen them enough to slip her hands out.

She was free!

But this was far from over.

Sadie pressed her hand over her wound, trying to slow the flow of blood.

As she did, she watched Carter and Emily walk offstage. She knew by the glance Carter gave her over his shoulder that he was doing this for her.

He wanted to get Emily away from her.

As much as Sadie appreciated his sacrifice, she couldn't let him do this.

All it would take was one wrong move, and Emily would snap.

Carter would be dead.

When the two of them were out of sight, Sadie grabbed the bottom of her T-shirt. Somehow, she managed to rip part of the bottom off. She tied it around her wound, stopping the blood flow —for now.

Then she dragged herself to her feet.

Rain still poured down, coming down harder than earlier. The water blurred her eyes, and the cool winds made her feel achy all over.

But she had to find help. There was no way she could help Carter alone, not in her current state.

Sadie grabbed the cell phone that had been tucked into her front pocket.

The lines were still down.

She needed a plan.

She stumbled toward the storage shed.

She needed to free Bo.

The dog let out a low growl. As he recognized her, his tail began wagging.

Sadie's head spun as she tried to untie him. But

she finally managed to undo the knot that kept the dog in place.

"We need to find them, boy," she muttered.

The dog barked, almost as if he understood.

Sadie gripped the rope around his neck, knowing she couldn't lose him.

The dog was smart. He could lead her to Carter.

The question was, would Sadie make it that far? Her wound still burned. Her shivers were uncontrollable. Her head felt woozy.

Moving as quickly as she could, she clambered through the sand until she reached the boardwalk. Bo pulled her to the north. That must be the direction Carter and Emily had gone.

Her head spun again.

Could she make it?

Sadie wouldn't be any good to Carter if she arrived only to pass out.

But how could she find help without a phone? No one else was crazy enough to be out here in these conditions.

A noise sounded behind her.

Her entire body tensed. She halfway expected Emily to be standing there with a gun.

Sadie spun around, vowing to fight with every last ounce of her energy.

"Sadie?" someone asked.

Cassidy came into view.

Sadie released her pent-up breath, nearly passing out with relief.

Finally, help was really here.

God had answered her prayers.

CHAPTER TWENTY-FIVE

CARTER GLANCED AROUND THE COTTAGE.
Pictures of him and Emily were everywhere. Pictures
of the two of them that had clearly been photoshopped.

More nausea churned in his gut.

This was even worse than he had thought.

"Do you like it?" Emily turned to him, still
holding the gun. She hadn't totally let down her
guard yet. But she didn't bother to hide her excitement either.

"I can't believe you did all this for me." The
words burned as they left his throat.

"I would do anything for you. Anything."

Carter stared at her, wondering if anything

would convince Emily to let him go right now. He had to keep her calm.

His thoughts went back to Sadie again. Was she okay? Had she found help yet? Had the bleeding stopped?

He had so many questions. All he wanted to do was to see Sadie. To make sure she was okay. To pull her into his arms and never let her go . . . in a romantic way, not in an Emily sort of way.

"Why don't you sit down and make yourself at home?" Emily pointed to the couch. "I'll get you something to drink."

Carter nodded, his throat tight as he slowly lowered himself onto the sofa. He'd seen Emily lock the doors behind her when they'd entered the cottage. Four locks had been there.

Even if Carter made a run for it, by the time he unlatched those, Emily would have drawn her gun and pulled the trigger.

He needed to think of another plan.

"I bought you another guitar." Emily's voice broke through his thoughts. "I thought maybe you could sing some songs. Won't that be fun?"

Playing for Emily? That didn't sound fun in the least. But it would buy him some time. "I . . . I always like playing songs."

"I know." Emily set a glass of lemonade in front of him and smiled. "We're going to be so happy together, Carter. So happy. Just you wait and see."

PARAMEDICS HAD QUICKLY BANDAGED SADIE. But she didn't have any time to waste. She would go to the clinic to be fully checked out—as soon as Carter was found.

She'd insisted that she go with Cassidy and two of her officers. Cassidy hadn't wanted Sadie to do so, but Sadie knew she might be one of the only people who could talk Emily down from the ledge. Otherwise, the results could be disastrous.

Her head was still woozy, but adrenaline fueled her actions. It would propel her to action until this was over.

Then she would crash. She had no doubt about that.

Sadie looked forward to that moment.

But only if Carter was with her. If something happened to him, she didn't know how she would go on.

She sat in the back of Cassidy's police SUV as they followed Officer Dillinger and Bo down the street. Officer Leggott drove behind them in his police cruiser.

The dog appeared to be leading them right to Carter.

Sadie prayed they got there in time.

She pulled the blanket Cassidy had given her around her shoulders. Sadie's clothes were still drenched. Still clinging to her. Her hair dripped down her back.

But she didn't care. Not right now.

Finally, the dog ran with Officer Dillinger to a little cottage set far off the road. As lightning flashed, Sadie could barely see a red Mustang parked behind some bushes in the distance.

This was it.

Bo had led them to Carter.

Sadie's heart raced at the realization.

Officer Dillinger appeared beside Cassidy's car. The police chief climbed out, and, a few seconds later, Bo hopped inside. Sadie reached up and rubbed the dog's face, murmuring a few words of praise.

Cassidy leaned into the car and locked her gaze on Sadie's. "Stay here."

"But—" Sadie started.

"There are no buts about it," Cassidy said. "I

shouldn't have let you come along. This woman is unstable, and you've already been shot once."

Sadie nodded, knowing she had no room to argue. The police chief's words made sense. But she wanted nothing more than to be out there and to do whatever she could to help.

She stayed true to her word and sat back in her seat, watching as Cassidy and her officers approached the house.

She prayed fervently that nobody would be hurt.

Especially not Carter.

CHAPTER TWENTY-SIX

"I BOUGHT SOME CLOTHES FOR YOU," Emily told Carter after he'd played three of her favorite songs. "Would you like to change? You must be so cold."

Carter's heart throbbed in his ears. This woman had even gone as far as to buy him clothing? Her words only confirmed how far from reality she was.

But maybe getting out of her sight for a moment would be good. Maybe this was Carter's opportunity.

Carter carefully set the guitar on the chair beside him. "I think that's a great idea. I'd hate to get sick on you. What good would I be then?"

"I would take care of you. Always." Emily smiled, as if delighted at the prospect. "I'll show you our room."

Our room? Carter swallowed hard. He didn't like the sound of that.

Emily kept the gun on him as they walked down the small hallway to the first bedroom.

"It's in here." She flipped on the lights. "Isn't it beautiful? I thought of you when I decorated it."

Images of his album covers decorated the walls. Emily had also made art using some of his song lyrics. The curtains were dark blue as well as the bedspread.

The place looked just like Carter's real bedroom at his apartment.

His throat tightened.

Had Emily seen it? Was that why she'd decorated this space this way?

Again, the thought didn't comfort him.

"The clothes are in there." She pointed with the gun toward the dresser.

Carter slowly walked toward it and opened the drawers. He pulled out a pair of jeans and a T-shirt.

They were his size.

"Thanks for these," he muttered. "I'll change now."

She nodded but made no effort to move. "Go ahead."

This wasn't going to work. Carter needed to be alone. Needed to clear his head.

"Could I have some privacy?" he asked.

She forced her eyebrows together. "But the two of us are together now. Why do you need privacy?"

He shrugged. "Maybe I'm a little shy sometimes."

Emily stared at him, and Carter wasn't sure if she'd believed his words. But after a moment, a satisfied smile stretched over her face. "That's right. You were a little shy in high school at times, weren't you? Until you got onstage. Then you were like a whole different person. That was just one more thing I liked about you."

He pointed to the bathroom attached to the room, not wanting to have this conversation with her. "Can I go in there and change?"

She didn't say anything for a moment until finally nodding. "I suppose so. We have the rest of our lives to get to know each other better."

Carter swallowed hard before slipping into the bathroom and quietly locking the door.

Once by himself, he leaned against the wall and tried to catch his breath.

How was he going to get out of this situation? He didn't have much time.

He dropped the clothes onto the floor and glanced around.

A window stretched behind the toilet. It was small. Like so many of the beach houses in this area, the structure was raised up on stilts. There was at least fourteen feet between that window and the ground.

But it might be worth it to risk the fall.

The storm would prove to be his friend right now. The sounds of the rain pounding against the tin roof overhead would obscure the noise of him opening the old window.

At least, Carter hoped so.

With the thought settled in his mind, he slowly pushed open the window.

It worked.

He shoved the screen out and watched as it fell onto the ground below.

Carter glanced down, realizing that fourteen feet was higher than he had envisioned.

Still, he would take his chances.

Just as he climbed on the toilet to make his escape, a knock sounded at the door.

"Are you okay in there, sweetie?" Emily asked. "How much longer?"

"Just one more minute," Carter called.

And then he jumped.

SADIE WATCHED as Cassidy and her officers surrounded the house. Any minute now, they should breach the front door. Sadie only hoped that Carter would be okay once they got inside.

She squinted as something else caught her eye.

Was that a fourth figure out there?

In the darkness, the movement was only a shadow.

Sadie held her breath, waiting for more lightning to illuminate the sky. She needed to see more details. Needed to know whether or not she should warn the officers.

Was it Emily? What if that woman had somehow anticipated that the police were coming, and she was headed out to counter their attack?

Sadie held her breath, wishing there was some way she could tell Cassidy what was happening. But the three of them were far away from the shadow. The phone lines were still down.

Making a split-second decision, Sadie opened the car door.

"Stay here, Bo," she muttered.

The dog whined.

"Sorry, boy. I don't want you to get hurt."

Bo let out another whine before laying down, his pouty eyes staring at her.

Remaining on the edges of the property, Sadie crept toward the shadow she'd seen. She needed a better look. If she had to, she could yell for Cassidy and alert her that an ambush was coming.

The shadowy figure headed toward the edge of the brush, where Sadie crouched.

Sadie sucked in a breath, unable to breath, to move, until she knew what was happening.

She definitely wasn't in the right state to defend herself now.

What would she do if this person found her? If this was Emily—and Sadie suspected it was—then the woman was unhinged *and* she had a gun. Sadie wouldn't stand a chance.

Sadie ducked behind a tree and hid.

Her fingers pressed into the smooth bark as a puddle of water climbed up her jeans.

Quietly, she waited. Her lungs felt like they'd been filled with sand.

She could hardly breathe.

A weapon! She needed a weapon.

She reached down and found a substantial branch. It was better than nothing.

As the figure crept closer, Sadie raised the branch above her head.

I don't want to use this, Lord. I'll probably only make Emily madder. But I can't stand here and do nothing.

Lightning flashed in the sky again.

As it did, the figure came into view.

It was . . . Carter.

Before Sadie could say anything, a shout sounded in the distance.

"You'll never get away!" someone yelled.

Emily. That sounded like Emily.

The next instant, gunfire filled the air.

CHAPTER TWENTY-SEVEN

CARTER FROZE as someone stepped from behind a tree.

Was he seeing things? Or was that . . . Sadie?

Her drenched figure appeared, surprise lacing her eyes.

A branch slipped from her hand as their gazes met.

"Carter?" she rasped, letting out a cry. "Is that really you?"

In two strides, he pulled Sadie into his arms. He couldn't believe she was here.

That she was alive.

That she'd come for him.

Just then, another bullet pierced the air. Carter shoved Sadie behind the tree and peered out.

"Is Emily shooting at us?" Sadie tensed in his arms, her breathing instantly becoming more labored.

Carter glanced back at the house he'd somehow managed to escape from. "It sounds like it. I jumped from the bathroom window. I hurt my ankle when I hit the ground, but I'll be okay."

"Cassidy and two of her guys are up there right now."

He held Sadie closer, wanting to guard her from anything else that might happen—both right now and in the future. She'd done so much for him. Now it was his turn.

"The police will take care of Emily," he murmured. "They're good at their jobs."

Sadie's muscles relaxed, just a little. She looked up at him, moisture like dew on her face but warmth saturated her eyes. "I was so scared for you, Carter. I thought—"

Carter tucked her head under his chin, unable to listen to the rest of her statement. "I was afraid Emily was going to kill you. I just wanted to get her away, to give you a fighting chance."

"Thank you for being willing to sacrifice your-self. But you didn't have to do that. You could have died."

He pulled back just enough to look Sadie in the eye. "Yes, I did. And I would do it again if I had the choice."

A sad smile tugged at her lips, and more moisture dripped from her face. This time, Carter felt certain those were tears. Tears of relief and happiness, he hoped.

As lightning flashed again, their gazes jerked toward Emily's house. The scene playing out on the deck filled Carter with relief.

Cassidy led Emily down the steps, toward her police SUV. The woman raged, yelled, thrashed.

But she also appeared to be handcuffed.

Carter wasn't sure what had happened up there, but it appeared this horrific ordeal was over.

Really over.

He turned back to Sadie, observing her and soaking in her features—this time without worry of Emily appearing to finish what she'd started.

Sadie's skin looked paler than usual, and moisture continued to run down her cheeks and nose.

As far as Carter was concerned, she'd never looked more beautiful. This woman was a true treasure to anyone who'd had the privilege of meeting her and getting to know her. Carter's life was certainly better because of her.

Carter lowered his lips to meet hers. She melted against him as their kiss deepened. It didn't matter that they were dirty. Drenched. Battered.

All that mattered was that he and Sadie were together.

When Carter finally pulled away, he lingered close enough for their foreheads to touch. "I love you, Sadie Thompson."

A grin spread across her face. "I love you too, Carter Denver."

SADIE CROSSED her legs as she sat on the couch in Carter's apartment.

A week had passed since everything had happened with Emily.

Cassidy and her crew had been able to breach the door at Emily's place, storm inside, and apprehend Emily. Even though the woman had a gun, the officers captured and arrested her without incident.

The sound of bullets that Sadie had heard was Emily leaning out the bathroom window and trying to shoot at Carter once she'd realized he'd escaped.

The woman truly had bought that cottage, the one that matched the lyrics of one of Carter's songs.

She'd been obsessed over Carter all these years, and all that craziness had bubbled over into the events that happened this last week.

Now that was over.

Praise God.

Emily was finally getting the help she needed and had been admitted to a psychiatric center. Specialists there would determine whether she was fit to stand trial. Either way, Sadie and Carter wouldn't be seeing her again for a long time.

Sadie's arm had been bandaged from where the bullet had grazed her. Carter's ankle had also been wrapped. He had a slight sprain from when he'd jumped from that bathroom window.

But things could have turned out so much worse. Sadie was grateful that they were both okay.

Carter sat down beside her on the couch and handed her a mug of coffee. "It's just the way you like it."

Sadie took a sip and smiled. "You're right. It is. Thank you, Carter."

He kissed the side of her head as he slipped an arm around her and pulled her closer. "No, thank you. Have I told you how glad I am that you're staying here in Lantern Beach?"

"You mentioned it a few times." She chuckled.

Carter actually mentioned that a few times *every day*. Sadie had no intention of asking him to stop. It was great to know that he shared her feelings, especially after all these years of being apart.

"I was thinking that after you did your podcast, the two of us could take a walk on the beach," Carter said.

"Is that such a good idea with your sprained ankle?"

"We'll just have to go slow. But we've always kept a good pace together."

She grinned again. "Yes, we have. A walk on the beach sounds great."

Carter pulled away just far enough to stare at her. The look in his eyes was pure gooey warmth that tempted Sadie far more than an ice cream sundae ever could.

"Are you sure you're going to be okay doing your podcast from here?" he asked.

Sadie nodded. "I found a place I can stay. I can set up my studio there. So much of my work is now done on the computer anyway. My consulting can be done with a webcam. In fact, I think this change will be good for me."

"What change in particular are you talking about? Being here on Lantern Beach?"

She smiled and rubbed the edge of Carter's face with her thumb. "No, being with you. That's all I dreamed about for years."

"Like Emily?" He raised his eyebrows in mock fear.

Sadie let out a quick laugh and backed away. "No. Nothing like Emily. But I was thinking about decorating one of the rooms in my new place with pictures that I've photoshopped of you and I together."

He shook his head and groaned. "Please, don't. But I would be happy to take some new pictures with you. Some real pictures."

Sadie grinned. "I would like that too. I think I'm going to be really happy here."

"I know I'm going to be happy now that you're here." Carter leaned toward her and planted another soft kiss on her lips. "I love you, Sadie."

"I love you too," she murmured. "A rainy day with you is better than a sunny day with anyone else."

He raised his eyebrows. "I think I feel a new song coming on."

She cuddled closer to him and smiled. "I can't wait to hear it."

~~~

Thank you for reading *Torrents of Fear*. If you enjoyed this book, would you leave a review? Reviews truly do help authors, and we appreciate them!

Catch up with all your favorite characters in an all new Lantern Beach series coming January 2020—Lantern Beach Guardians.

If you haven't signed up for my newsletter yet, please do so here: www.christybarritt.com.

COMPLETE BOOK LIST

Squeaky Clean Mysteries:

#13 Cold Case: Clean Getaway

#14 Cold Case: Clean Sweep

#15 Cold Case: Clean Break

#16 Cleans to an End (coming soon)

While You Were Sweeping, A Riley Thomas Spinoff

The Sierra Files:

#1 Pounced

#2 Hunted

#3 Pranced

#4 Rattled

The Gabby St. Claire Diaries (a Tween Mystery series):

The Curtain Call Caper

The Disappearing Dog Dilemma

The Bungled Bike Burglaries

The Worst Detective Ever

#1 Ready to Fumble

#2 Reign of Error

#3 Safety in Blunders

#4 Join the Flub

#5 Blooper Freak

#6 Flaw Abiding Citizen

#7 Gaffe Out Loud

#8 Joke and Dagger

#9 Wreck the Halls

#10 Glitch and Famous (coming soon)

Raven Remington

Relentless 1

Relentless 2 (coming soon)

Holly Anna Paladin Mysteries:

#1 Random Acts of Murder

#2 Random Acts of Deceit

#2.5 Random Acts of Scrooge

#3 Random Acts of Malice

#4 Random Acts of Greed

#5 Random Acts of Fraud

#6 Random Acts of Outrage

#7 Random Acts of Iniquity

Lantern Beach Mysteries

#1 Hidden Currents

#2 Flood Watch

#3 Storm Surge

#4 Dangerous Waters

#5 Perilous Riptide

#6 Deadly Undertow

Lantern Beach Romantic Suspense

Tides of Deception

Shadow of Intrigue

Storm of Doubt

Winds of Danger

Rains of Remorse

Torrents of Fear

Lantern Beach P.D.

On the Lookout

Attempt to Locate

First Degree Murder

Dead on Arrival

Plan of Action

Lantern Beach Escape

Afterglow (a novelette)

Lantern Beach Blackout

Dark Water

Safe Harbor

Ripple Effect

Rising Tide

Crime á la Mode

Deadman's Float

Milkshake Up

Bomb Pop Threat

Banana Split Personalities

The Sidekick's Survival Guide

The Art of Eavesdropping

The Perks of Meddling

The Exercise of Interfering

The Practice of Prying

The Skill of Snooping

The Craft of Being Covert

Saltwater Cowboys

Saltwater Cowboy

Breakwater Protector (coming soon)

Carolina Moon Series

Home Before Dark

Gone By Dark

Wait Until Dark

Light the Dark

Taken By Dark

Suburban Sleuth Mysteries:

Death of the Couch Potato's Wife

Fog Lake Suspense:
  Edge of Peril
  Margin of Error
  Brink of Danger
  Line of Duty

Cape Thomas Series:
  Dubiosity
  Disillusioned
  Distorted

Standalone Romantic Mystery:
  The Good Girl

Suspense:
  Imperfect
  The Wrecking

Sweet Christmas Novella:
  Home to Chestnut Grove

Standalone Romantic-Suspense:
  Keeping Guard
  The Last Target
  Race Against Time
  Ricochet

Key Witness

Lifeline

High-Stakes Holiday Reunion

Desperate Measures

Hidden Agenda

Mountain Hideaway

Dark Harbor

Shadow of Suspicion

The Baby Assignment

The Cradle Conspiracy

Trained to Defend

Mountain Survival (coming soon)

Nonfiction:

Characters in the Kitchen

Changed: True Stories of Finding God through Christian Music (out of print)

The Novel in Me: The Beginner's Guide to Writing and Publishing a Novel (out of print)

HIDE AND SEEK: LANTERN BEACH GUARDIANS

When Cassidy and Ty find a child on the beach, mute from an unknown trauma, they begin a search for her family. Clues washing up from a shipwreck reveal few details about what might have happened. But, as they uncover more, Cassidy and Ty discover something that has more far reaching implications than they ever imagined . . . and now it's a fight to save everything they love.

Preorder your copy HERE.

ABOUT THE AUTHOR

USA Today has called Christy Barritt's books "scary, funny, passionate, and quirky."

Christy writes both mystery and romantic suspense novels that are clean with underlying messages of faith. Her books have won the Daphne du Maurier Award for Excellence in Suspense and Mystery, have been twice nominated for the Romantic Times Reviewers' Choice Award, and have finaled for both a Carol Award and Foreword Magazine's Book of the Year.

She is married to her Prince Charming, a man who thinks she's hilarious—but only when she's not trying to be. Christy is a self-proclaimed klutz, an avid music lover who's known for spontaneously bursting into song, and a road trip aficionado.

When she's not working or spending time with her family, she enjoys singing, playing the guitar, and exploring small, unsuspecting towns where people have no idea how accident-prone she is.

Find Christy online at:
    www.christybarritt.com
    www.facebook.com/christybarritt
    www.twitter.com/cbarritt

Sign up for Christy's newsletter to get information on all of her latest releases here: www.christybarritt.com/newsletter-sign-up/

If you enjoyed this book, please consider leaving a review.

Made in the USA
Middletown, DE
24 August 2024

59665710R00135